CLOCKSTOPPERS

CLOCKSTOPPERS

A novelization by ROB HEDDEN and ANDY HEDDEN
Based on the story by ROB HEDDEN & ANDY HEDDEN
and J. DAVID STEM & DAVID N. WEISS
Screenplay by ROB HEDDEN and J. DAVID STEM & DAVID N. WEISS

SIMON PULSE
New York   London   Toronto   Sydney   Singapore

First Simon Pulse edition March 2002

™ & copyright © 2002 by Paramount Pictures and Viacom International Inc. All Rights Reserved.

SIMON PULSE
An imprint of Simon & Schuster
Children's Publishing Division
1230 Avenue of the Americas
New York, NY 10020

Design by Ann Sullivan
The text of this book was set in A Garamond
Printed in the United States of America
10 9 8 7 6 5 4 3 2 1

The Library of Congress Catalog Card Number: 2002100291

ISBN: 0-7434-4222-9

FOREWORD

Clockstoppers was born from the mind of a seven-year-old. While on vacation one summer, my eldest son Ryan sat in the backseat of our rental car, rambling on about the exploits of a character named "Professor Idiot" as he ignored the scenery outside. I asked him on what TV show he'd seen this professor. "I made him up," he answered, adding that his imaginary character invented all kinds of wacky things.

The name stuck in my head, and maybe six months later, my brother Andy and I collaborated on a story about a professor, his son, and an invention called a molecular accelerator.

Six years and plenty of rewrites down the road, *Clockstoppers* has been made into a motion picture. While the name "Professor Idiot" was changed along the way, the original inspiration survived intact.

Besides thanking Ryan, we will always be indebted to science teacher John Wilkerson and the students at Thurston Middle School in Laguna Beach, California, for allowing us to pick their brains during the research phase. We also offer our grateful thanks to the talented writers who contributed to the final shooting script, as well as the filmmakers who brilliantly brought it to life, especially our good friend, director Jonathan Frakes.

—Rob Hedden

CLOCKSTOPPERS

ONE

The large clock appeared to be broken, its second hand stopped at thirteen seconds past the hour. It had a plaque beneath it with two words: LOS ANGELES.

It wasn't the only timepiece on display inside the Bradley Terminal at Los Angeles International Airport, which for some reason was eerily silent. New York, London, Paris, Moscow—every time zone across the globe was represented. And just like Los Angeles, every single one was frozen in time.

Suddenly all the clocks began to tick in perfect synchronicity. At the same moment, the din of travelers rushing to make their flights flooded the terminal. High heels clicked over the shiny marble floor. Luggage wheels clattered onto escalators. Time had abruptly resumed.

Dr. Earl Dopler was among the throng, pushing his way through the International Departures terminal to the ticket counter. Barely thirty and arguably a genius, the bearded, longhaired man in the crumpled Hawaiian shirt looked more like a surfer than a scientist. Dopler nervously glanced upward at the clocks through his sunglasses, struggling to keep his frayed duffel from sliding off his shoulder.

Dopler was in more of a rush than most, with good reason. He had something that powerful people wanted. He glanced backwards constantly, as if they were not far behind.

"I'm sorry, sir, but the two o'clock to Costa Rica is completely booked," said the clean-cut airline ticket agent with a plastered-on smile.

"Come on, man, you can stick me in cargo!" barked Dopler, loud enough for everyone in line to hear.

The agent calmly entered keystrokes into his terminal. "I could put you on the eight-oh-five," he offered with the identical smile.

"Not if I'm dead you can't."

Dopler hurried off, wiping his long blond hair off his sweaty forehead as he sprinted toward the departure gates.

BEEEEEEP.

A burly security officer blocked Dopler as he blew through the metal detector and set off the alarm.

"Please empty your pockets and pass through again, sir," ordered the imposing officer.

Seeing that it was fruitless to argue, Dopler

quickly emptied his pockets. Loose change and a miniature "8-ball" key ring fell into the plastic tray. He rushed through again.

BEEEEEEP.

Dopler sighed, doing a quick back step. He threw an anxious glance over his shoulder and then quickly unstrapped his wristwatch.

At first glance, it appeared to be an ordinary dive watch with a Day-Glo yellow bezel. On closer inspection, one could see that the brand name had been replaced with the initials "QT," framed within an elaborate futuristic logo.

Dopler passed through the scanner again. No alarm this time. He quickly scooped up his watch and launched toward the gates.

"Sir, you forgot your keys!" called the officer.

"Keep 'em!" Dopler yelled back, without breaking stride.

He made it to gate 43B, where an electronic display above the counter confirmed it was flight 1433 to Costa Rica, scheduled to depart on time. Dopler scoped out the sardine-packed waiting area. He spotted an empty seat beside a balding middle-aged tourist in a loud hibiscus-print shirt. Dopler slid into it, caught his breath, and quickly made the man an offer.

"Care to sell your ticket?"

"Are you nuts?" uttered the balding guy.

"Look, man, I need a vacation *real* bad," pleaded Dopler, unable to stop fidgeting. "I'll pay you double for it."

"My wife's waited her whole life for this trip," countered the tourist, more than a little incensed.

Dopler glanced at the man's frazzled wife, who was doing her best to entertain their three-year-old boy and twin baby girls. Dopler sympathized with her, but his life was on the line. He quickly unzipped a pouch on his duffel and pulled out a thick wad of hundred-dollar bills. He stuffed them into the tourist's hands.

"Ya think she can wait a little bit longer?"

The tourist gazed at the fistful of cash, easily double the amount he was spending on their entire trip.

One minute later, Dopler was standing in the boarding line with a ticket firmly in his grasp. He did his best to block out the sobbing of the tourist's wife as they left the airport with their twins and screaming toddler. Dopler glanced at his QT wristwatch, praying the seconds would pass more quickly. He fumbled for a roll of antacids from his shirt pocket and downed half of them. He was now only one step away from handing over his boarding pass and stepping onto the 737. Dopler tried to control his breathing and his thudding heart. He was actually going to get away.

Two seconds later, people began yelling behind him.

Dopler turned with dread, just in time to see the impossible. Travelers and their luggage were being knocked over like bowling pins by an invisible force . . . rolling directly toward *him*.

Completely freaked, Dopler instinctively reached for his watch.

As if by magic, right before his eyes, it vanished off his wrist.

Dopler let that register for a scant second before bolting ahead in line, his hand outstretched with the boarding pass like a relay runner passing off a baton. As the flight attendant reached to take it, the pass disappeared from his hand in a blink.

Dopler's jaw barely had time to drop before he felt himself being yanked backwards, as if by powerful ghosts. He screamed futilely as his tennis shoes screeched across the slick terminal floor at an impossible velocity. To all who observed, Dopler was barely visible. After all, he was moving in excess of three hundred miles per hour.

The speeding blur that was Dopler streaked out of the terminal and slammed into a waiting gray van. As the door magically slid shut, the same QT logo as on Dopler's watch came into view on the van's side.

Dopler panted hard inside the vehicle. He gazed around to find he was alone. He lunged for the doors, but they were electronically locked. He was a prisoner.

The van abruptly began to vibrate with a low *whirr*.

Dopler knew what this meant. He forced himself to turn around.

Henry Gates was now seated opposite him, having materialized out of thin air.

"Well, if it isn't the famous Dr. Dopler," said Gates, with feigned pleasantness.

Gates had a jaw that didn't look like it would break, no matter how hard you slugged him. He was in his late thirties and striking, with steel-edged cheekbones and a weathered face that had seen military duty. Gates wore a slick gray business suit that matched his eyes.

"You know, you're never going to win employee of the month if you keep running off like this," Gates said coolly. He grabbed Dopler's long sandy hair and yanked it hard. It was a wig, covering short brown hair matted with perspiration. Gates then ripped off Dopler's fake beard, taking some skin with it.

"Oww!" cried the scientist, jerking his head in pain.

Dopler now noticed that Gates was not alone. Sitting behind the wheel was an imposing man named Richard, one of Henry Gates's "associates." Richard's job qualifications included having biceps that could barely be contained inside his size 48 jacket.

In the passenger seat sat a businesslike woman, Gates's head of security. Her name was Jay. What she lacked in size, she made up for in shrewdness. Jay dangled Dopler's wristwatch just out of reach with a taunting smile.

"Stealing company property is a big no-no, Doctor."

Dopler's expression sank to a new low.

"I think it's time you came back to work," Gates said in a voice that held no compromise.

Dopler's mouth went dry. His life would be over very soon.

TWO

Zak Gibbs impatiently waited opposite the red light, the front wheel of his tricked-out BMX bicycle kissing the crosswalk. With both feet on the rear wheel pegs, Zak straddled the black alloy frame and adroitly balanced the motionless bike. Helping him concentrate was the music fed to his ear-buds via the MP3 player in the pocket of his vintage bowling shirt. With warm brown eyes, dark chestnut hair and a boy-next-door smile, the seventeen-year-old was immediately likeable.

The signal turned green and Zak pedaled off, zigzagging through the small town intersection. Hopping a curb, he took a shortcut through the town square and deftly negotiated the venerable trees and manicured flowerbeds. He rolled up to the Curious Wonders thrift shop, sliding his cycle into the bike rack and locking it. Zak wasn't there to buy a specific item—he never was—but he always seemed to find exactly what he wanted. He briskly cruised the jam-packed aisles, stacked ceiling high with what most people would call junk. Rusted hubcaps. Swag lamps. Waffle irons with frayed cords.

His vision fell on a turquoise transistor radio. Zak lifted the dusty device, not much larger than his MP3 player but decades older. He popped out his ear-buds and thumbed the radio's round black dial, clicking it on. It made noise, mostly static with a hint of AM music. He nodded to himself.

Minutes later, Zak was pedaling down the appropriately named Oak Avenue toward his home. Afternoon sunlight filtered through the tree-lined street, splashing a few rays on a neighbor's curbside trash barrels. Several boxes of junk were piled next to the recycle bin. Zak flew past it, and then skidded to an abrupt stop.

His keen eyes had spotted an old black typewriter on top of the heap. He circled the battered manual Royal a second time, as if he were a fine art collector examining a Monet. Even if the ancient writing machine no longer functioned, it could still be worth something, he thought. Zak swooped in and hoisted the cumbersome beast under his left arm, pedaling off.

He was home less than three minutes later and went straight to his bedroom with his newly acquired treasures. Zak's home was an inviting single-story house with oak floors and lots of stained glass. His bedroom had a view of the back rose garden, though he rarely noticed it. Like most days after school, Zak's eyes were on a monitor, his fingers nimbly entering keystrokes into his desktop PC. Soon he was logged on to eBay.

Zak lifted a digital camera cabled to his computer and snapped a quick photo of the transistor radio. Using a pillowcase as a backdrop, he had isolated it on his desk as if he were shooting a fancy product shot, complete with backlighting from his halogen desk lamp.

Within seconds an image appeared on his screen, a reasonably flattering product shot of the antique radio. *"PRICELESS RELIC FROM BEATLES ERA—MIN. BID $10"* appeared beneath the photo as Zak typed it in.

The old Royal also had its turn in the limelight, with Zak revising its initial description from *"ANTIQUE TYPEWRITER"* to *"CRASH-PROOF WORD PROCESSOR."* The flashier description inspired him to increase the minimum bid from five dollars to twenty-five.

Zak Gibbs was nothing less than resourceful. It was part of his nature. Today he was especially motivated, had been for the last two weeks, in fact, ever since he saw the cherry-red 1965 Mustang convertible sitting on the lot at Benson's Used Cars. His freshly awarded driver's license was burning a hole in his wallet, but more than that, he'd wanted this car ever since he was seven, when his dad had given him a model kit of the classic car for a birthday present. In fact, it was the first model he and his dad had ever built together. The Mustang held a prominent spot on top of his monitor, with a dozen other elaborately painted models sharing desk space—everything from cars to battleships to the Creature from the Black Lagoon.

As Zak logged off the Web, his eyes rose to the toy Mustang. Prophetically, it was the same color red as the one he'd seen for sale at Benson's, right in his hometown.

Zak wanted that car more than anything in his life.

"Let's look at another example," said Professor George Gibbs as he addressed close to fifty wide-eyed college freshmen. His attention shifted to a girl with short red hair, feverishly taking notes.

"Let's say Amy's out for a nice leisurely drive in her Honda Civic," lectured the professor, "and Eddy comes screaming by in a brand new Ferrari." The class tittered. The Eddy in question was a long-haired slacker who severely lacked ambition. If Eddy was driving a Ferrari, he probably stole it.

"What?" croaked Eddy with a start. He'd been napping up to the point his name was spoken.

Professor Gibbs now had the undivided attention of his entire class. A handsome forty-five with no hint of gray in his thick dark hair, he was highly respected in the academic community. This was due to his teaching ability, to be sure, but it was also due to the rapport he had with his students. It was common knowledge that Dr. Gibbs had launched the career of many a distinguished scientist, and was a brilliant researcher in his own right.

"Okay, Amy, so you're doing twenty in your Honda, and Eddy comes racing by at *two hundred and twenty*," continued Professor Gibbs. "What's he going to look like as he goes by?"

"I don't know, pretty much a blur, I guess," offered the redhead.

"Exactly," praised Dr. Gibbs. "In fact, if Eddy were going fast enough, you wouldn't see him at all. And to him, *you* would seem like you're standing still."

Most of the class nodded with understanding. The professor turned to Eddy, who was glancing out the window at a Tony Hawk–wannabe skateboarding past the classroom.

"What I've just described is a basic example of Einstein's theory of *what*, Eddy?"

The slacker turned away from the window.

"Uh . . . highway safety?"

A few snickers told Eddy he was probably incorrect. Professor Gibbs half-smiled, but he was not amused. He wanted to get through to each and every one of them.

"People, science is a discipline. Our department has trained some of the best minds in the world, but nobody ever got there by coasting along."

At that moment, Zak coasted up just outside the professor's teaching lab.

"I don't mean to sound like your father,"

continued Dr. Gibbs, "but I take pride in my students and I like to see them succeed."

He saw Zak sneak in the back door just as he finished the sentence.

"That means doing the work, being persistent and not always looking for the quick fix or the easy way out," concluded Professor Gibbs, his eyes on his son the entire time. After an awkward moment, he turned back to the class.

"All right, we'll finish up with Einstein when I get back from the Applied Science Convention next week. Meanwhile, you've got a few days off . . ." The students immediately applauded. ". . . to study for your midterm," he finished. Groans replaced the clapping.

As the class filed out, Zak found his way down to his father's podium. Professor Gibbs looked up with a small smile as he collected his lecture notes.

"Hey, Zak, this is a rare honor," he said with a hint of strain.

"C'mon, Dad, I visit you at work now and then." Zak was also a bit uncomfortable.

"Uh-huh, but a careful analysis reveals it's usually because you need something."

"That's crazy," Zak replied a little too defensively. It was probably because he knew there was a bit of truth to it. Especially now. "Can you come with me to co-sign for my car? I got the down payment together."

Professor Gibbs sighed as he walked from the lecture hall, Zak right on his heels.

"Dad, there's a car down at Benson's lot that's just, well, *perfect*," continued Zak, his voice involuntarily rising. "They stay open till nine tonight, so if we could just . . ."

"Jere!" his dad called out, waving at a pinstriped administrator crossing the campus. "Where's my stipend on the NASA consultation? We finished that job three months ago!"

"Workin' on it, George!" replied the administrator, adding details that went in and out of Zak's ears without registering. As soon as the two men had concluded the exchange, Zak broke in.

"So Dad, if we get there by seven, we could—"

"Hey, Dr. Gibbs, your batch is up on the mainframe," interrupted a tall grad student who breezed past them. "Some pretty wild stuff, Professor."

"Thanks, Sam," Dr. Gibbs offered with a smile. "I'll be right down."

Zak was getting frustrated. *Maybe I jumped into the car thing too quickly,* he thought. He decided to try a different approach.

"What are you working on, Dad?" In truth, he *was* curious about his father's work. Although most of his dad's research was boring, occasionally he was involved in some fascinating and downright bizarre experiments.

"Oh, last week an old student sent me a project he's developing for QT Laboratories," replied Professor Gibbs, who seemed pleased that his son was interested. "You remember Earl Dopler—one of the brightest students to ever come through here."

"That freak who used to blow things up in the school lab?"

"He's not a freak," defended the professor. "A little eccentric, maybe, but . . . anyway, his project is hush-hush."

"You can't tell me *anything* about it?" coaxed Zak.

Professor Gibbs hesitated, but he couldn't resist. What Earl Dopler had sent him was beyond exciting.

"Well, let's just say, hypothetically, that it was possible to accelerate your molecular structure to the point that the rest of the world seemed to be standing still."

"I'm not sure I get it."

"It's called *hypertime*," continued Zak's father, elated by the mere possibility of it. "Your molecules are moving so fast that you're invisible, yet through your eyes, time is moving so slowly that it appears to have stopped."

"Cool," replied Zak. It *was* cool.

"Imagine being able to perform delicate surgery between the beating of a heart," enthused the professor. "This technology could revolutionize medicine, science, travel. . . ."

"Hey, speaking of travel, I really want to make this car thing happen tonight."

Zak didn't mean to blurt it out, but it seemed like a good place to change the subject.

"Right," exhaled Gibbs, his enthusiasm drifting off like smoke. Zak was there because he needed something, and it wasn't a physics discourse. "Did you download the *Consumer Reports* like I asked you?"

"Oh, um, yeah, I was going to do that before you came home," Zak stammered. "C'mon, Dad, you already blew me off last week."

"I didn't blow you off, I got called in on a student meeting with the dean."

"And *that's* never happened before." Zak was letting his emotions get the better of him. Yes, he was annoyed. But he was also hurt by his father's lack of attention.

Professor Gibbs appraised his son for several moments. He truly loved Zak. Sometimes he found it difficult to show this, especially with all the distractions of his career.

"All right, do your homework on this—let's see those safety reports."

Zak's face lit up. "Does that mean we can go tonight?"

"It means we'll talk when I get home."

"Yes!" exclaimed Zak, taking it as a bona fide affirmative. He gave his dad a quick hug and hopped on his bike, flying off across the campus. His dream of owning the Mustang convertible was about to come true, and nothing was going to stop it from happening.

THREE

THWACK!

A bright yellow splotch of paint exploded against Meeker's smock as the paintball hit him, fired by a gleeful twelve-year-old.

"It's very safe, and a great father-son activity," said the athletic young saleswoman. She was standing with the boy's dad just outside the paintball gun demo booth at X-Dream Sports, where Meeker Smith worked. A lanky high school senior with cornrowed brown hair, Meeker winced as the little commando squeezed off a final shot that smacked him squarely in the butt.

The kid howled with delight as he dragged his father past the snowboard and skateboard displays to pay for the gun.

Zak stepped into the booth as his paint-

_____ _____ dental
_____ to endure. He always tried his
_____ geekiness, but couldn't quite succeed.

"Whazzup, Zak?"

"Check it out."

Zak fanned a dozen checks. Meeker took them, staining a couple with yellow thumbprints.

"Dude, you made all that just by selling junk on your computer?"

"One man's junk, another man's down payment," beamed Zak. "You got to start thinking outside the box, Meeker."

"What box?"

"The box you're in that keeps you from seeing that this five-dollar-an-hour job blows."

"Yeah, well, I'm not gonna be here forever," Meeker replied. "Check this out—PLUR 102 is having a DJ contest tomorrow night and I'm signed up." He handed Zak a flashy flyer from his back pocket. PLUR 102 was a very happening club, an industrial-strength dance palace with no age restrictions.

"Underground dance par-tay," Zak said as he perused the flyer. "How Dr. Dre of you."

"I've been practicing," boasted Zak's bud. "I sneak away from study hall and work the turntables in the tech room."

Zak missed the last few words. His attention had been diverted to the climbing wall just outside X-Dream's front door.

"Whoa . . . who is *that*?"

His eyes had fallen on Francesca Cava, a stunning sixteen-year-old beauty with waist-length black hair. She was wearing khaki climbing shorts and a cream tank top, which contrasted perfectly with her mocha-colored skin. Francesca was about to scale the climbing wall.

"Ooooh," smirked Meeker. "Where have you been, Zakster? That's Francesca, the new girl from *Venezuelaaah*."

"She goes to our school?" Zak said with disbelief. "Now that's gotta be good for attendance."

"Tell me about it. She has P.E. when I'm in band. I get smacked every time the trombones turn to look at her."

"Oh, this is too sweet," uttered Zak, the wheels turning.

"Whaddaya mean?"

"Foreign girl in a foreign land . . . all lonely and vulnerable," he mused out loud. "I read all about this in *Cosmo*."

Despite the big talk, Zak was truly captivated by the beautiful girl, and more than a little intimidated.

"I gotta go talk to her," he said, working up the nerve.

"You are gonna get so *faaaced*," warned Meeker.

"Watch and learn," he replied, trying to sound more confident than he was.

Francesca was halfway up the climbing wall as Zak stepped outside. He squinted up at her,

Francesca's lithe figure rimmed in the afternoon sun. Her beauty, as well as her agility, mesmerized him. He searched for the right words.

"Excuse me, do you have the time?"

Francesca peered down at him, her expression telling Zak what he already knew: It was an utterly stupid question. With both her hands clinging to the rope and her feet precariously wedged into the faux rock, how could she possibly check the time? Not only that, she wasn't wearing a watch.

"Uh . . . I mean, uh, don't you go to my school?" he quickly added, but it was a lame recovery.

"I couldn't say," she said with an obvious accent. "What school is yours?" Her voice was as smooth as her skin.

"Jefferson," he called up to her. "My friend watches you in P.E."

She gave him a look.

"I mean, you're new, right?" He winced.

"Oh yes," she answered liltingly. As Francesca descended toward him, his confidence began to rise.

"Well, I'm Zak . . . and I was thinking maybe I could show you around? I mean, I know how lonely it can get when you move to a new town."

"Yes. *Que bueno*. It is so very hard."

She was now face-to-face with him. Her irises were deep brown with flecks of gold, like tiger's-eye gemstones. Zak was now officially infatuated.

"I try to be brave, exploring the town all by myself," she cooed, then her expression changed.

"When all I really want is to give my love to the first BOZO who wants to know the time."

Zak felt his brain go numb.

"I read *Cosmo*, too," Francesca sneered, in perfect English with zero hint of an accent. She gripped the rope again and climbed out of his life.

Zak just stood there, feebly watching her ascend.

"Right. Okay, then. I'll, uh, see you around."

It fell on deaf ears. Nevertheless, he already knew he wouldn't be able to get this girl out of his head.

FOUR

"**A**re you watching this?"

Kelly Gibbs had one hand on a flip phone, the other gripping a TV remote.

"He was so cute, and now he's all, 'I'm a gangsta, *yo*.'"

The precocious twelve-year-old blonde watched the rapper on cable for another two seconds, then exiled him in favor of another station. With her trendy purple jacket and orange satin pants, Kelly could've been in a music video herself.

Zak frowned at his little sister as he paced into the family room. He was holding a cordless phone as he ogled the newspaper classifieds.

"I was in earlier today about the Mustang," he said anxiously into the receiver. "You've still got it, right?"

He held his breath. Then closed his eyes with relief.

"Great—I'll be there tonight with the down payment."

He disconnected and strode into the kitchen, where his mother was busy removing a stack of frozen entrees from the microwave. Zak watched as she happily scooped the steaming stroganoff and buttered broccoli from their cardboard containers into festive serving bowls.

"What are you doing, Mom?"

"This way it's like homemade," she beamed as the slimy noodles slid down the bowl's sides. With the sweetest of smiles and brightest of eyes, Jenny Gibbs seemed to be perennially cheerful. "I want us to have a nice family meal together before your father goes off to his science conference."

Zak's face drained.

"But he's taking me to buy a car as soon as he gets home."

"After dinner," corrected Mrs. Gibbs. She handed the bowl to her son, motioning for him to place it on their oak dining table.

"Mom, can I have some money?" pleaded Kelly, still armed with the cell phone and remote.

"Did you do your chores?"

Kelly wavered. She turned to Zak, her voice turning honey-sweet.

"Have I told you lately how much I respect and admire you?"

"Hmmm," weighed Zak, holding out his palms

as if they were a set of scales. "Buy a car? Or give money to Satan?"

Kelly lifted the phone to her glossed lips and groaned to her girlfriend. "You're so lucky you're an only child."

Kelly was just going through her "me" phase, figured Zak. She was only twelve; she'd eventually grow out of the teen-pop wardrobe and cellular attitude, he told himself. But that didn't make living with her now any easier.

Those thoughts were banished the second he heard the front door open.

"Hey, Dad!"

Professor Gibbs stepped over the threshold, loaded down with a briefcase too stuffed to close. Zak hurried over.

"Mom says we can head out after dinner, which is cool 'cause we can still make it by nine."

"Make what?"

Dr. Gibbs was exhausted from a day of teaching and labs. Before Zak could refresh his memory, a stack of his data fell onto the floor. Zak picked it up without skipping a beat.

"The car lot—they've got the '65 Mustang I told you about, a four-speed with a V8," he gushed. "*Consumer Reports* rated it a Best Buy. . . ."

Professor Gibbs was glancing at a printout that Zak had just returned to him. The document triggered thoughts of work he had yet to accomplish.

"It has good reliability, decent gas mileage and reasonable crash-test scores, you know, for a convertible," finished Zak, trying to sound responsible.

His father looked up from his data. "Okay. And what else did you compare it to?"

"Nothing," Zak replied matter-of-factly. "This is the car I want."

"Zak, you can't prove your case by just ignoring all the other data."

Zak couldn't believe his ears. What had happened to his father, the man who had once helped him build a replica of the very car he now wanted to buy?

"Dad, it's not a clinical trial. When something's right, you've got to close your eyes, grit your teeth and go on faith."

"No, you've got to step back, weigh the options and make a calculated choice," Dr. Gibbs lectured. "Now do your homework on this, and if you still want the Mustang when I get back, that's what we'll get."

"Dad, this car will be gone by next week!" Zak forced himself to keep his voice from rising. "At least come and look at it."

"When I get back. I've got to look over Earl Dopler's project tonight—I promised him."

"Oh, I get it," said Zak with realization. "So *that's* what this is about. It doesn't have anything to do with me looking at other cars."

"What are you talking about?" countered his father.

"Nothing . . . it's just . . . you've always got time for your students, but you don't have time for your own kids."

"Hey, I asked you to come with me to the conference," his father pointed out defensively. "Who was the one who was too busy then?"

"Oh yeah, 'The Congress of Applied Science'— now *there's* big fun for the whole family." A second after the words left his tongue, Zak wished he hadn't said them.

"All right you two, time out," chirped Mrs. Gibbs as she carried out the rest of dinner. "Sit. Eat. Some of the greatest peace treaties in history have been signed over stroganoff and buttered broccoli."

Zak stared at his father. "Thanks, Mom . . . I'm just not hungry."

Professor Gibbs had lost his appetite as well. He didn't like disappointing Zak, but he had made a promise to Dopler. He was also trying to teach his son some important life lessons.

"Zak, I promise, as soon as I get back we'll go straight down to—"

"Tell it to your students," interrupted Zak. He stormed into his bedroom and closed the door.

Zak stared at the little Mustang on top of his monitor. He was beyond upset, feeling he'd lost all chance at getting his dream.

Buttons and zippers clattered inside the clothes dryer.

Professor Gibbs was too absorbed to notice as he dissected an intricately constructed device about the size of a quarter. During the decade that the Gibbs family had lived in their home on Oak Avenue, the basement had slowly changed from laundry room to laboratory. The makeshift workbench was piled high with disassembled appliances, memory chips and electronic paraphernalia of dubious origin.

The professor attached tiny alligator clips to the coin-sized mechanism. Wires attached to these clips disappeared behind a black mid-tower CPU, which had a 21-inch hi-def monitor perched above it on a homemade pine shelf. Mathematical equations were screaming across the screen at a blinding rate.

Dr. Gibbs nudged the bridge of his glasses up his nose and leaned in for a closer look at the gadget, which had begun to glow. Tiny laser lights, no thicker than a thread, were pulsating beneath its translucent housing.

He jotted some notes on a yellow legal pad just as his wife walked in with a mug of peppermint tea.

"I don't know how you work in this mess," she said, trying to clear a spot on his bench. She gave up and tossed an old chrome toaster in the waste-basket, then set down the tea.

"What are you doing? I was going to fix that for you," her husband objected.

"Sweetheart, I bought a new toaster a year ago."

Mrs. Gibbs smiled good-naturedly, surveying his organized chaos. She spotted a colorful brochure amidst the electronics and lifted it. "What's this, George?"

"My itinerary for the conference," he said with-out looking up. "Why don't you hang onto it so you'll know where to reach me?"

"Why don't you leave it with Zak?"

He met her eyes as she handed it back to him, guilt tugging hard.

"I know . . . I don't want to go off with things bad between us either," he said finally. "It's just . . . he's got so much potential, and yeah, right now he can just skate by, take all the shortcuts. But it's going to catch up with him."

"Maybe," she answered, "but he's still finding his way, George. And just because it's not your way doesn't mean he's lost."

Professor Gibbs sighed. She was right.

"Let me just put this thing back together and I'll go make peace."

"Don't forget," she cautioned. "You know how you get caught up down here."

"Two minutes—I promise." To show good faith, he shut down his computer.

Mrs. Gibbs kissed him on the forehead and left. He lifted the tiny device that had swallowed the better part of his evening and gave it a final, curious look. He then snapped it back into a familiar housing—a dive watch that featured the QT logo on its bright yellow bezel.

Professor Gibbs was analyzing an exact replica of the wristwatch Dopler was wearing when he was abducted.

Zak was stretched out on his bed, his MP3 player drowning out the evening's disappointment. Though he didn't hear the knock, he glimpsed his door opening from the corner of his eye.

"Hey," said his father, tentatively stepping into the doorway.

Zak reluctantly removed his ear-buds.

"Hey."

There was an awkward silence before Dr. Gibbs spoke again.

"So . . . anything you want to talk about before I go?"

Zak glanced at the digital clock on his night-stand. It was 9:01. The car lot had just closed.

"Nope. I'm good," he said evenly. *Actually, I'm just great,* he thought. *Red '65 Mustang convertibles show up on Benson's lot all the time, at least once a millennium.*

Professor Gibbs knew his son was upset, but he didn't grasp the magnitude of Zak's disappointment. "All right. Well, I guess I'll be going then."

Zak didn't reply. Dr. Gibbs wanted to say more, lots more, but the words eluded him. He awkwardly turned to leave, then remembered the flyer.

"Oh, here—in case you need to get in touch with me, or if you decide to come visit." He handed Zak his conference itinerary. "It's going to be a lot of fun, and—" He stopped midsentence. His son's sarcastic comment about the conference being "big fun for the whole family" still stung. "Whatever you feel like doing, Zak."

Zak took the itinerary without comment, setting it on his desk beside the Revell X-15 rocket that he and his dad had glued but never got around to painting. It was the last model they had worked on together.

"Have fun with your science friends," said Zak.

Professor Gibbs smiled back weakly, then left the room.

The following morning, Kelly was having her usual fashion crisis as she rifled through the dryer in search of a clean halter top. Clothes were flying everywhere, most of them landing on her father's workbench. She spotted a splash of hot-pink Lycra tangled around a pair of faded jeans. Kelly grabbed the jeans and sent them into orbit as she retrieved her top. Unfortunately, the jeans landed on a shoe box that was precariously balanced on the shelf above the workbench. The box came tumbling down, spilling its electronic contents everywhere.

"Mom!" shouted Kelly. "Zak's pants knocked over Dad's stuff!"

Kelly didn't notice the small label on the box, which had two handwritten words on it: DOPLER PROJECT. Nor did she see that the QT wristwatch, a device that would change the world, had fallen into a small white microwave oven awaiting Professor Gibbs's tinkering.

A half hour later, the microwave was sitting in a big cardboard box on the kitchen counter. Mrs. Gibbs had written DONATE TO GOODWILL across the side with a marker. A broken blender and other curios from the basement were piled beneath it.

Mrs. Gibbs started to carry the heavy box toward her station wagon in the driveway.

"Hey!" called Zak, downing a slice of cold toast in preparation for first period. He grabbed a green rubber antenna protruding from the box, extracting an ancient G.I. Joe walkie-talkie. "Dad fixed that for me so I could sell it."

The plastic housing immediately fell apart in his hands, springs and wires flying everywhere.

"Figures," he mumbled, tossing the toy back. He was still hurting from the night before.

"You know, when your father's old and gray, you're going to regret not having a better relationship with him," Zak's mother said in a somber tone that was out of character.

"Yeah, well, there's plenty of time for that." Zak lifted the Goodwill box so his mom wouldn't have to carry it.

Three steps later, something caught his eye. A luminescent-green digital display was winking back at him through the glass door of the microwave.

Zak set down the box. He reached inside the oven, retrieving the QT wristwatch.

"Cool," he said to himself, pocketing it.

FIVE

Zak was pedaling along the sidewalk adjacent to the cafeteria at Jefferson High. Meeker and he had just come back from a fish taco lunch in town, an off-campus privilege earned by seniors if they maintained a 3.5 average or higher. Meeker was on a skateboard that thoroughly qualified as custom— Birdhouse deck, Darkstar wheels and Bullet bearings. Ultra-hip transpo, to be sure, but it still didn't eliminate his dork factor, especially with the trombone case tucked under his arm.

"I got some phat pants and a wicked shirt," Meeker said as he grabbed onto Zak's bike seat and hitched a ride. "This DJ thing is gonna be so fresh." Meeker popped a baby pacifier into his mouth, trying to look as "phat" as possible. Zak glanced back at him and grimaced.

"That's it. Let go of the bike, Meeker."

They coasted onto the lunch patio just as Kurt Ditmar shoved his way out the cafeteria doors. Ditmar, universally known as "Dit-O," was a rock-star wannabe with spiky blond hair and a serious attitude.

"Oh man, here we go," moaned Meeker, quickly spitting out the pacifier.

Dit-O had a friend in tow named Jocko, who had long dirty hair and was decked out in an XXL tie-dyed shirt and tent-sized pants similar to Dit-O's. The pair was lunching on vending-machine chimichangas and soft drinks. Needless to say, they didn't qualify for the off-campus privilege.

"Hey, Freaker!" yelled Dit-O when he spotted Meeker. "Was I trippin' on some bad lunch meat or did I hear you signed up for the spin-off tonight?"

"Lay off him, Ditmar," warned Zak.

"Yo, I ain't *on* the freak. . . . " Dit-O immediately contradicted his statement and got in Meeker's face. "But listen here, Meek-man, tonight it's gonna just be me and you onstage. You ain't gonna have your sister here backing you up."

Meeker held his ground. "What was that you said? 'Cause all I can hear is the crowd, and they're yelling, 'Go, Meeker, Go Meeker . . .'" He launched into what he thought was a slick strut, but it looked more like a comedy routine.

"Oh! He's on fire!" howled Dit-O. "Somebody better cool him down!" Ditmar shook up his bottle of soda and sprayed it in Meeker's face. Jocko cracked up.

"Later, Jerk," dismissed Dit-O as he and Jocko bailed. Dit-O tossed the empty plastic bottle toward a barrel. It missed but he didn't bother picking it up.

Zak was embarrassed for his friend, but sometimes Meeker was his own worst enemy.

"What'd I tell you about Cabbage-Patching in public?"

Meeker made no comment as he blotted the sticky fizz off his face with his shirt. Zak just shook his head.

He didn't notice that Francesca had witnessed the whole exchange as she walked across the patio.

As Zak locked his BMX to the bike rack, he heard the Shady Duo making loud catcalls. He looked up and saw Dit-O and Jocko swooping in on Francesca.

"Hola, Chiquita, I'm Dit-O—I'm spinning at an underground tonight. Wanna come?"

The lovely Venezuelan ignored him. Dit-O grinned at Jocko, the blow-off only spurring him on. Both boys followed her and continued their harassment.

Zak watched them, his blood beginning to boil. Meeker followed Zak's gaze, but he wasn't thinking about Francesca. If Meeker lost the spin-off, he'd never hear the end of it.

"Seriously, man, you're not gonna leave me hanging out there alone tonight, are you?"

"I'll be there," answered Zak, his eyes focused

on Dit-O and Jocko. A second later, he marched toward them.

"What's the matter, *no habla Ingles*?" taunted Dit-O. Francesca continued to disregard his presence until he grabbed her arm. She abruptly stopped near a gaggle of students and faced Ditmar demurely. She was actually a couple of inches taller.

"Is hard," she lilted in her fake accent, even thicker than the one she had used on Zak, "but I try to watch and learn. Like this, for example . . ." Francesca shook up her soda and sprayed Dit-O in the face, totally drenching him. "Later, Jerk," she said, dropping her accent.

The crowd laughed hard, including Jocko. Ditmar wiped the caramel-colored droplets from his eye sockets, regaining his vision. He gazed at Francesca hatefully. She was not intimidated.

"Excuse me, make a hole," said Zak, pushing his way through the crowd like a prince determined to save his damsel.

"Sure, here's a hole for you—"

He couldn't tell if it was Dit-O or Jocko who said it, but *both* of them heaved him into a trash can. Drink bottles and fast-food cartons spilled everywhere.

"Hey, hey!" shouted Mrs. Deakins, the plump, business-suited vice principal. "That's a perfectly good trash can! Don't go throwing students at it!"

Dit-O and Jocko instinctively dispersed at the presence of authority. Zak nonchalantly extricated himself from the garbage. He brushed away a burrito wrapper stuck to his shirt as Francesca approached him.

"I didn't need any help," she said.

"Huh? Oh, um . . . my friend lost his retainer," he lamely offered, gesturing at the trash. "Guess it's not here."

She looked over at Meeker, who smiled back obliviously. The retainer was still clamped to his gums.

"Very nice. Now, if you'll excuse me . . ." Francesca tossed her empty bottle into the trash. It was a swish shot.

Zak watched her go. Twice he'd let her get away now. Just before she disappeared into the science wing, he made a decision. "Hey, listen, while I've got you here . . . I'm sorry I was such a dip yesterday."

She stopped and faced him. "Only yesterday?"

Zak slowly closed the gap between them.

"No. Everyday. I'll apologize for global warming if you'll give me another chance. Cup of coffee after school?"

"I have plans."

"How about after your plans?"

"I have more plans."

"Would it be such a stretch for some of your plans to include me?"

She studied him. He was persistent, but in a charming way. He was sweet, too, and kind of funny. She noticed his big brown eyes for the first time. Francesca felt her face flush and was mad at herself.

"All right . . . I guess we can all use a second chance."

Zak felt a wave of something he couldn't quite describe wash over him, pooling somewhere in his stomach. The anticipation doubled as she turned him around and used his back as a writing surface.

"Here's my address," she said, scribbling it onto her notepad. "I have to baby-sit my little brother and sister today, so, come by around four?"

"Four . . . yeah . . . I'm good then." He would've come at four in the morning if that's what she'd wanted.

"Great. I'll see you then." She smiled at him for the first time as she handed him her address. Her teeth were white and perfect. Her whole face glowed.

There was nothing left to say, so they went their separate ways. As soon as she was out of view, Zak did a little victory dance.

Two hours later, Zak gazed at the classroom clock in seventh-period geography, just as he'd done in his fifth- and sixth-period classes. *Almost there.* The time he'd spent anticipating the arrival of four o'clock had been the longest two hours of his life. It felt like time was moving slower than a snail.

SIX

Francesca and her family had just moved into a sprawling Spanish-style hacienda in the historical section of town. A red tile roof covered the second story, with white stucco walls and landscaped terra-cotta walkways shaded beneath it.

Zak approached the arched front door and felt dwarfed by its size. To say he was nervous was a sizeable understatement. He took a deep breath, swallowed hard and tapped the big iron knocker.

Ten seconds passed, which seemed like ten hours. Finally, the heavy door swung open, revealing Francesca in a sheer floral skirt and pink halter top. She gave him the best smile of his life for the second time that day.

"So, I thought maybe we could spend some time by the pool while the sun's still nice, okay?" She hadn't planned on speaking first, but Zak had been rendered mute.

"Great, catch some rays," he offered when his brain kicked in. "That works."

She led him through her foyer, which was as warm and tasteful as the exterior. Large pastoral paintings hung over Old-World antiques. It seemed like Zak had been transported to another time and place, yet he felt right at home. Francesca guided him across her expansive living room and through a set of French doors that led to the patio outside.

The backyard was practically a park, with rolling lawns, lush flower beds and a swimming pool shaded by tall elms. Francesca's ten-year-old sister Rosa waved at them from a tree swing in the far corner of the yard. The view was reminiscent of a painting.

Zak drank in the sublime setting, ready for an afternoon in paradise.

"There's another rake over there," said Francesca as she grabbed one by a tree. Zak followed her glance to a nearby toolshed. It was then he noticed the thick layer of leaves covering her huge lawn. Having raked literally tons of leaves for a dollar an hour in junior high, Zak never wanted to see a rake again in his life.

"Uh, right. See, when I said 'another chance,' I was thinking a cup of coffee or maybe dinner and a movie?"

"I told you I had plans. *You* asked if they could include you."

She had him there. "Yeah, I guess I did."

"Look at it this way," she explained. "You go to the movies, you can't have a conversation. You go for coffee, there's always a lull. This way, when there's a lull, my leaves get raked."

"And you're going to rake all these leaves by hand?" He was still not sold on doing hard labor.

"My father says it develops self-discipline."

"That's what they always say when they want you to do stuff for free."

Zak looked around the yard at the daunting task ahead. His eyes fell on an old riding mower beside the shed. The inventing gene he'd acquired from his father sparked to life.

"Got an idea . . ."

Ten minutes later, Zak had duct-taped a section of pool sweeper hose to the exhaust pipe on the mower. He'd created a very functional leaf blower and was quickly accomplishing Francesca's mission. As he rode around the yard and blew the leaves into large piles, Francesca scooped them into garbage bags. She was duly impressed.

Zak was smiling the whole time. He had never enjoyed yard work more in his life.

"And then, when I was fifteen, we left Caracas for London, but just when I was making friends my father was transferred here," Francesca yelled over the mower-turned-blower.

"Wow, you've lived all over," he shouted back. Zak turned off the mower and helped her bag the leaves. "My dad took us to Lego Land once—it has the Eiffel Tower and the Taj Mahal."

She laughed easily. He loved that she laughed at his jokes.

"Don't feel bad . . . at least you actually have a place to call home," she said in a tone that revealed the first signs of vulnerability.

"I guess," he quietly answered. "But it must be cool to be a consul's daughter. That makes you, like, royalty, doesn't it?"

"Oh yeah. I'm just waited on hand and foot." She hoisted two bags and moved toward the shed. Zak followed her with two more. Francesca frowned as the trash barrels came into view. Two cans had been knocked over, garbage everywhere.

"Aah! I'd like to catch the dog that does this!"

She leaned down and started to clean up the mess. "So much for making us some cappuccino."

"Cappuccino?" he grinned. "Don't we have to wash your car or paint the house first?" In truth, he would have gladly done all of the above for her. The afternoon was passing way too quickly—he'd have to go home soon.

"No, that's next weekend," she laughed. Zak was definitely growing on her. She didn't want the afternoon to end either.

"Tell you what—you start the caffeine and I'll finish up out here," he offered.

"Really? Great. Then maybe we'll still have time for a swim. What time is it?"

"I don't know," he said, since he wasn't wearing a watch.

But then he remembered.

"Wait . . ."

He dug into his pocket and extracted the QT wristwatch. The luminescent-green display was fully functioning with a digital readout. "It's, um, 16:57, whatever that is."

"Almost five. I'd better get going." She grinned and walked toward the house.

Zak beamed. He couldn't remember feeling this good ever. He glanced at his new watch again. That morning he'd planned on offering it up to the eBay gods, but now, on closer inspection, he decided to keep it. Zak strapped it on and pressed a few buttons on its bright yellow bezel to test all of its functions.

His thumb found a button on the left side and squeezed it.

A powerful wave of energy suddenly engulfed him. Although Zak could not fully describe the exact sensation, it was as if he rippled for an instant.

Zak shook his head, trying to clear the dizziness. Fortunately, it passed as quickly as it came. He glanced down at the watch again.

"Whoa."

The numbers were screaming across its display in a green blur. Assuming it had a stopwatch function that had gone haywire, Zak tried to shut it off. After pressing several buttons with no effect, he gave up and bent down to pick up the trash.

The neighborhood had gone eerily silent. Behind him, Francesca's sister Rosa was still on the swing, her dark hair fanned out as she pumped into a high arc.

Zak was facing away from her. He didn't see that she was literally frozen in mid-flight.

SEVEN

It took Zak close to twenty minutes to finish cleaning up the yard. Lost in his thoughts, the prevailing silence didn't fully register. *It's a really quiet neighborhood*, he thought in passing, but any deeper scrutiny was swallowed by visions of swimming with Francesca.

Rosa had moved a couple inches in the swing since Zak pressed the watch button, but she was still, essentially, stopped in time. Zak probably would have noticed her if she had been moving at a normal speed, but his daydreaming kept his eyes off that corner of the yard.

He lifted the last bag of leaves and carried them to the shed.

"Yaaaaah!" A possum was staring back at him,

atop one of the trash cans. "Get out of here, you big rat—go on, shoo . . ."

It didn't budge.

Zak grabbed a small branch from the refuse and cautiously poked at the animal.

Still nothing.

"Seriously, don't make me kick your butt."

Zak foisted the branch harder, jabbing the possum in the side. The creature toppled over, as if it were stuffed. "Whoa."

At this same moment, Francesca was in the kitchen, standing opposite an espresso maker. She had just begun to prepare their cappuccinos.

Francesca was as static as a mannequin. Not a single muscle on her body was in motion.

Zak didn't see her as he entered through the French doors. He was holding the inanimate possum by the tail.

"Hey Francesca! I found your troublemaker!"

She didn't answer. He drew closer to the kitchen, his view of Francesca blocked by cupboards.

"I don't know what you guys are throwing away, but I think it gave this little guy a heart attack."

As he stepped into the kitchen, the QT wristwatch began to *beep* and drew Zak's attention. AUTO RETURN ENGAGED filled the display.

That same rippling sensation washed over him again. The sound of the refrigerator humming, of birds chirping outside, of a car driving by, crashed into his consciousness.

As did Francesca's screaming.

"Eeeaaahhhh!"

The possum was 100 percent alive and wriggling in his grasp, trying very hard to sink its teeth into Zak's arm.

Zak howled as he flung the nasty marsupial onto her kitchen island. Francesca screamed even louder and launched into a diatribe in Español. Though her words were unintelligible to Zak, he had a pretty good idea she wasn't happy.

The possum now had her cornered, so Zak did what any brave suitor would do. He grabbed a pair of salad tongs.

"Get him out! Get him out!" she screamed.

"He was dead! I swear he was dead!" Zak tried to explain as he kept the monster at bay with the tongs.

"I don't care—get rid of him!"

At least she was back to English, Zak thought between tong jousts.

Not waiting for Zak to rescue her, Francesca grabbed the spray nozzle from the sink and fired it at the possum. The soaked creature leapt off the counter and scurried out the door, but not before shattering a vase.

Zak surveyed the mess, as well as Francesca's furious expression.

"What is wrong with you?" she exploded.

"I'm sorry—I really thought he was dead." He wondered if she was this hot tempered all the time.

"We were having such a good time!" she fumed. "I can't leave you alone for two seconds?"

"Two seconds? I've been out there for almost half an hour!"

"Half an hour? I just walked in here!" she shot back.

Zak had no immediate comeback. He glanced at his watch.

"That's weird." The display had changed again. HYPERTIME EXPOSURE: 29 MINUTES filled the crystal. "Hypertime exposure . . . ?" He was utterly puzzled.

So was Francesca, but for different reasons. She had assumed Zak was different, but he was shaping up to be a typical male.

"Look, maybe you should just go."

"Go? What about swimming?"

Zak fiddled with the watch as he spoke. Somewhere in the recesses of his memory, he recalled a conversation he'd had with his father. Something about *hypertime*.

"You want swimming? I'll give you swimming . . ."

She grabbed the spray nozzle and pulled the trigger.

At the exact same time, Zak pressed the left button on the watch.

Once again, he rippled briefly. But this time he didn't notice the dizziness because he was too busy flinching in anticipation of being soaked.

Strangely enough, he was perfectly dry.

Zak rubbed his eyes with complete disbelief. Francesca was as still as a statue, her eyes flared. A stream of water sprayed from her nozzle, but it had stopped inches from his face, frozen in tiny crystal droplets.

"No way . . ."

He stared long enough to confirm he wasn't dreaming. Zak lifted his wrist and glanced at the watch. Time was passing by in a digital blur again.

"No way . . ."

He stepped around the airborne water droplets and stood beside Francesca. He waved a hand in front of her face. She had zero reaction.

"Francesca?"

She couldn't hear him either. Standing this close to her, he began to appreciate her unbelievable beauty.

"You have nice skin," he said out loud, leaning closer. A cloud of guilt abruptly engulfed him.

"All right, stop, you're creeping me out," he whispered to himself. Zak took a long look at the watch. He had almost figured out how it worked. Zak pressed the button on the left side again.

He vibrated for less than a second as normal time resumed. The nozzle spray kicked in like a fire hose and soaked the cupboard directly behind where Zak had been standing.

Francesca let go of the trigger, her brown eyes widening. How could Zak be standing right beside her? It was as if he'd beamed himself out of the spray's path in less than a heartbeat.

"How'd you do that?"

"I'm not really sure," he slowly responded. In truth, he *was* kind of sure. Zak peered at the watch, the QT logo glinting back at him. He knew beyond a shadow of a doubt that the watch had inexplicably caused this.

"All right, I don't know what you're up to, but out you go," she said angrily. Francesca took him by the arm and started to show him out.

"No, wait! Something weird's going on!"

"You and your big rat! That's what's weird!" she launched back.

"I swear, I'm not trying to freak you out!" he pleaded, the front door coming up quick. "It's just that when you started to spray me, I pressed this button, and—"

Zak pressed the button again as she swung the door open. Sure enough, he began to ripple . . . but this time, so did Francesca. She was still gripping his forearm as the vibration traveled up Zak's arm and into her body like a low voltage shock, the process occurring in milliseconds.

Francesca felt light-headed, but after a few deep breaths she felt fine again, at least physically. *Mentally* was a whole different matter.

"*Hay Dios,*" she barely whispered as she gazed out the front door.

What she saw defied logic. Water from the sprinklers hung in frozen droplets. A pair of sparrows were flying by, their fluttering wings captured in still-motion like a photograph. Francesca's thirteen-year-old brother Paulo was scooting into the backyard on his scooter, suspended in midair as he jumped a flowerpot.

"This is what I've been trying to tell you," uttered Zak.

She drank in the surreal tableau for another few seconds, not bothering to rub her eyes. This was really and truly happening.

"You . . . did this?"

"I think it's the watch." Zak stared at the glowing display again, the numbers screaming by. "My dad consults on all these super-secret projects and I think this is one of them."

She didn't question it as she stepped out the door, like Alice stepping into Wonderland. Francesca soon discovered, as Zak had learned, that her little brother could not see or hear her. She hurried around to the backyard and found Rosa in the same state on the swing. A squirrel hopped across a branch directly above her sister, also locked in time.

"So, your watch . . . stops time?" she said it matter-of-factly. It was such a preposterous notion, why try to sugarcoat it?

"I guess so," he replied. Zak was standing next to a yellow rosebush. A bee was hovering just above a blooming flower, frozen like everything else.

Or was it?

"Wait a minute. Look—he's moving."

Zak was right. The bee's translucent wings, normally invisible in flight, could be seen in intricate detail as they fluidly beat up and down in ultra-slow motion. And now that he looked around, the birds were moving as well. Just like the bees, it was almost imperceptible.

Disparate items in Zak's brain began to make a connection. His attention again returned to the watch. He focused on the logo.

"QT. . . . *QT*? That's where Dopler works. Quantum Tech."

Francesca said nothing, still fascinated by the honeybee. Zak began to pace. His father did the same thing when he tried to think.

"This must be the thing my Dad was helping Dopler with—Dad said something about it accelerating your molecules so fast that the rest of the world would seem like it was standing still."

Zak looked at the yard, at the whole world, with a new realization.

"I don't think time has stopped. I think we're just moving *really* fast."

Francesca moved toward the sprinklers. She reached out to touch the crystallized spray, leaving behind a perfect imprint of her hand.

"Look at this," she uttered with total amazement. Francesca cautiously stepped forward and walked through the spray, carving out a body-shaped tunnel as she passed. The droplets that touched her body rolled down her bare shoulders, but the rest remained dead still.

As she came out the other side, her eyes fell on her swimming pool. The blue-shirted pool man was removing leaves from the surface, his sweeping motion creating perfectly formed waves that looked like ice sculptures.

"How come I sped up and he didn't?"

Zak had no quick answer. He moved in front of the pool man. "I'm not sure. Let's see."

Zak activated the watch and the world slammed back into real time. The pool man shouted with shock—through his eyes, Zak had appeared out of nowhere. The poor guy lost his balance and fell into the deep end.

Zak turned back to Francesca. She was nowhere to be seen.

"Francesca?"

At the split-second time had resumed, Francesca had apparently disappeared into thin air. He had left her in hypertime.

Zak turned around. "Aaaaah!!!"

Francesca's brother Paulo, who had been frozen the previous moment, was now flying directly toward Zak, two seconds from putting scooter tracks across his chest.

Zak instinctively pressed the watch button and Paulo literally freeze-framed, stopping inches from Zak's face.

"It's about time."

The voice belonged to Francesca. She was reclining in a chaise lounge at poolside, reading a copy of *Cosmo*. Though less than ten seconds had passed in real time, she'd been relaxing there for over an hour.

The pool man was now re-frozen in the deep end, a look of terror etched on his face as he floundered. The chlorinated water cascading off his arms looked like crystal stalactites.

It just keeps getting weirder, thought Zak. He refocused on Francesca, trying to make sense of what just happened.

"I guess I left you behind."

"Don't do it again," she said half-jokingly.

"I guess for this thing to work, we have to be touching."

"Uh-huh," she said knowingly. "Sooner or later, all guys say that."

Zak peered down at his arm. The full ramifications of what he had strapped to his wrist began to sink in.

Francesca sidestepped the pool edge to meet him. She looked down and saw ripples slapping the tile edge in ultra-slow moving time. The watch's awe-inspiring power had not been lost on her either.

"What now?"

It was a question Zak had already been contemplating. "Well, you know, with such awesome power comes awesome responsibility."

She gave him a dubious look.

"That's what my dad would say, anyway . . . but he's not here, is he?"

A mischievous smile crossed his lips. There was an entire world out there standing nearly dead still . . . . and he planned on exploring every inch of it.

EIGHT

The charming downtown square was bustling with traffic and pedestrians. It was Friday afternoon and many people were just getting off work or arriving for a weekend getaway. Patrons flowed in and out of shops. College kids packed the local coffee shop. Children tossed coins into the town center fountain.

The lively village scene suddenly came to a grinding halt as an invisible force rippled over the town. Traffic, people, tossed pennies, all of it, stopped in mid-motion.

A bicycle moving at normal speed came into view, weaving its way through the inert landscape. Zak pedaled in front of an imposing city bus that under normal circumstances would have flattened him. Francesca clung to his shoulders, her feet balanced on the back pegs of his bike. The wind created by their movement made her skirt and hair dance, but everything else was still.

They rolled up to a bike rack on Main Street. Zak didn't bother to lock up; there was no need in hypertime. They took in their surroundings, wonder and mischief competing in their minds.

"Where do we start?" Zak finally asked.

Francesca had an answer almost immediately.

"Agh, there's that woman who's always giving me parking tickets."

A uniformed meter maid in her forties with permanent frown marks was standing opposite a parked car, scrawling out a citation. Francesca stepped closer and eyed the meter. It still had two minutes of time remaining.

"Look at her, she writes them before the meter even expires!"

Zak put his hands on his hips in mock disgust. "She has offended my sense of justice!"

He thought about it for two seconds, his creative juices flowing. Zak lifted the slight woman and carried her back to her three-wheeled police cart. She was now giving *herself* a ticket.

Francesca admired his work, but Zak was still unsatisfied.

"It needs something more . . ."

He looked around and spotted a mangy short-haired mutt lifting his leg on a curbside tree. Zak smiled devilishly.

A few minutes later, Francesca and Zak were

standing beside a crying toddler, his tears drifting in midair. The two-year-old was holding an ice cream cone, looking at the ground. Both of his chocolate scoops were resting in the dirt.

"Poor little guy."

"You take care of him," said Zak, "and I'll take care of *them*."

His vision had drifted into an alley beyond the bench. A pair of high school dropouts who had been voted "Most Likely to be Incarcerated" were living up to their potential. The one with the scraggly beard was busy tagging the wall behind Curious Wonders, Zak's favorite thrift store. The other, who sported a nose ring, was attempting to steal a mountain bike that belonged to one of the shop's employees, a guy Zak knew.

Zak approached the tagger first, marveling at the micro-droplets of paint misting from the canister's nozzle. By now, Zak had a reasonable grasp of the physics involved in hypertime, and quickly conjured an idea. He turned the can of spray paint in Scraggly Beard's grip until it was pointing in the opposite direction.

He then stepped over to Nose Ring Boy, who had just about severed the bike lock with a pair of bolt cutters. Zak kneeled beside the slacker, whose shifty face was only inches away from the rear wheel spokes.

"Nice nose ring," he smiled.

When their handiwork was complete, Francesca and Zak rendezvoused at the center of town. Zak took one last look at the silent, unmoving city that stood before them.

"You ready?"

Francesca placed her hand on Zak's shoulder so they would be in contact. "Make it so, Number One."

Zak gave her a look.

"What? We have *Star Trek* in Venezuela."

As Zak raised his wrist, he did feel like Number One. The feeling of power was intoxicating. He pressed the bezel button.

A shockwave that only the two of them felt rolled over the town as real time resumed.

"Oh! Oh! Oh! Oh!" It was the meter maid, who thought she'd lost her mind. "Aaaaaah! Get out! Get out!"

Not only was she giving herself a ticket, a mongrel dog was standing on her seat, peeing all over her steering wheel.

The meter maid wasn't the only one in town shrieking.

"Aaaaaaaaaaaaargh!"

Scraggly Beard flew out of the alley. The can of paint had ended up pointed at him, spraying his clothes with multiple coats of glossy blue enamel. Totally freaked, he ran up Main Street, right past the toddler who'd lost his scoops. The little kid had stopped sobbing. Courtesy of Francesca, a five-gallon drum of chocolate ice cream had instantaneously appeared in his lap.

"Nice touch," complimented Zak.

A moment later, shouting could be heard from the alley.

"Hey, man, don't leave me here!!!"

Though his bearded bud was long gone, Nose Ring Boy was still in the alley. The would-be bike thief was on his knees beside the mountain bike, chained to one of the spokes through his nose ring.

Zak and Francesca were pleased with their work. He glanced at his watch as it caught the last traces of sunset, his respect for the device rising exponentially.

"We're gonna have some *serious* fun with this thing."

QT Laboratories was an innocuous, low-rise facility. The discreet logo at the gated entrance gave no hint as to what transpired inside. This was exactly how Henry Gates wanted it.

"Look, Mr. Gates, I don't make policy, but I do enforce it."

Agent James Moore of the National Security Agency was sitting at the black granite conference table in Quantum Tech's executive chambers. With charcoal walls, no paintings, and dim illumination from wall sconces, the room was dark and oppressive. Just like its owner.

"They're shutting me down?"

Gates was strangely calm. He and Agent Moore, a no-nonsense man in his fifties with a crew cut, were the only ones occupying the huge space.

"Hey, you knew it was a Black Ops contract," said Moore.

Black Ops was short for "Black Operations," which was governmental doublespeak for top-secret, ultra-classified, "If I Tell You I'll Have to Kill You" projects.

"The Administration found out about the Clockstoppers project and they want it to go away," added the NSA agent.

Like all megalomaniacs, Gates had zero interest in governmental dictums. He was his own government.

"What can politicians possibly understand about what we're doing here?" he eventually responded.

"Gates, I supported you on this as long as I could, but they've got a point," answered Moore. "What if this device fell into the wrong hands? Fact is, someone could waltz right through an entire army and we would be useless to stop him."

Gates took a measured pause. He wanted the lie he was about to tell to sound sincere.

"Well, thank heaven they pulled the plug before we actually *built* one of the things. Why, I could've sold it on the black market for a fortune."

Agent Moore studied him. Little did he know that a half-dozen fully functioning prototypes of the watch were already in Gates's possession. Gates was wearing one, even as they spoke.

"Mr. Gates, the NSA expects your research, your equipment—the whole shooting match—crated and ready for pickup on Monday."

"And if I'm not ready?"

"We're taking it whether you're ready or not."

Agent Moore offered no departing smile as he exited. An NSA chopper was resting on the rooftop helipad just outside the conference room, awaiting his departure.

Within seconds of the chopper lifting off, Gates was striding down a long metallic corridor. He was accompanied by his strong-arm, Richard, and the lovely but lethal Jay. Glass partitions beside them revealed supercomputers busily crunching numbers. Gates and his associates reached the end of the hall, which dead-ended into a lone elevator.

WHOOSH.

The elevator door opened vertically. Gates, Richard and Jay stepped inside, the door sliding down again like a guillotine. Gates stiffened his index finger and stabbed a button in the panel labeled LEVEL THREE.

"Restricted access requested," came the synthetic female voice. *"Please step forward for retinal scan."*

Gates placed his right eye against the retinal scanner that was built into the access panel. A laser scanner briefly spilled across his pupils, then disappeared.

"Have a nice day . . . Henry Gates."

The elevator began to descend. The QT Laboratories that the public saw aboveground was just the tip of Gates's top-secret iceberg. Hidden below ground was a sprawling research facility.

WHOOSH.

The elevator door pneumatically rose again as they arrived on level three—the nerve center of QT

Laboratories. A massive metallic grid work criss-crossed the four-story-high interior. Research stations were located on three different levels, crammed with the latest in computer hardware and monitoring systems. Large white tanks filled with liquid nitrogen flanked the walls on every level.

While all of this was impressive, the focal point of the room was a towering glass and steel structure known as the "Clean Room." The vaulted conical chamber was airtight, its windows two inches thick. Inside, more nebulous technology was on display. However vague their functions were, one fact was clear—many, many millions of the taxpayer's dollars had been sent Gates's way.

A pair of QT technicians guarding the Clean Room entrance immediately rose upon seeing Gates.

"How's he doing?" Gates's voice was level. If Agent Moore had put a chink in his armor, he didn't betray it.

"Seems okay," replied the lab-coated technician.

Exactly whom they were discussing was unclear, as the Clean Room appeared to be empty.

"But," added the technician, "he wrote *that* about half an hour ago." He pointed at a dry-erase board inside the Clean Room. Complicated equations were scrawled across it, along with—

YOU'RE KILLING ME . . .

"How dramatic," Gates said with no pity whatsoever.

Then, in a flash, it became—
YOU'RE KILLING ME . . . *NIMROD*.

"And charming," added Gates. "All right, bring him down."

The QT technicians went to their stations and entered keystrokes. There was a hiss of rushing gas as liquid nitrogen flooded into the Clean Room through ceiling vents.

As the temperature began to drop, a flurry of movement began to materialize. A chair was careening around the room at a zillion miles per hour. Pencils, paper and a coffee mug were moving on a drafting table at light speed. Sketches and equations were magically written and erased and rewritten, all in a blink. Finally, a blurry human shape appeared, speeding about the chamber like a pinball. As more liquid nitrogen engulfed the room, the shape finally slowed, then stopped, then collapsed in a chair.

The man had ice on his clothes, the extreme cold having slowed his molecules down from hypertime into real time.

"Hello, Dr. Dopler," Gates said cheerfully. "How are things in hypertime?"

The icy man turned around. Dopler still had on his Hawaiian shirt, yet he now looked twenty years older, with thinning gray hair and prominent crow's feet around his eyes.

"How are things in *hypertime*?" cracked Dopler's voice. "Look at me, man! I've been in here a week and it's like I've aged a couple decades!"

"Yes, but see how productive you've been?"

retorted Gates. "Not to mention all the vacation you've accrued."

"Aw, man . . . why don't you just kill me now?"

Although Dopler was worn out, he was still lucid enough to know that Gates wouldn't kill him, at least not until he had solved the "big problem" involving hypertime. The big problem was, in fact, the glitch that had dramatically aged Dopler.

"I was hoping that wouldn't be necessary," replied Gates. "Besides, it's your own fault. If you had solved the aging problem in the original design, we wouldn't have had to bring you back."

The Clean Room door opened and Gates entered, ignoring the cold. He immediately pressed a button on the metallic wall. A hydraulic *hum* sounded as a circular platform rose from beneath the floor at the center of the room.

A huge flat panel monitor was perched atop the platform, illuminated with a computer-modeled 3-D drawing. The image resembled a futuristic dentist's chair of sorts, with cranial scanners and a complicated control panel. ION STABILIZER was labeled above it.

"Yeah, well that's the thing, man," said the shivering Dopler as he stared at the computer graphic. "The ion stabilizer *should* be able to reverse the aging effects in hypertime. But, uh, I'm having a little trouble with the programming, and . . ."

"Earl, the NSA wants all our toys in three days," interrupted Gates.

"Hey, well, they're their toys, Chief."

"They don't know the watches exist yet, and I

have no intention of turning them over," Gates said firmly. "But how am I going to enjoy the power of hypertime if I'm going to end up looking old, like *you*?"

Dopler rubbed his icy arms, feeling as old and cold as he looked.

Gates peered at the ion stabilizer on the monitor again. "You have forty-eight hours to get this thing working."

"That's impossible, man."

"Then I guess I *will* have to kill you."

Gates nodded to Richard and Jay, who moved in quickly and dragged Dopler from his chair. It could've been a bluff, but Dopler was in no condition to call it.

"Aw, wait, man! Maybe I could do it faster—there's some data I'm waiting on from a friend!"

"A *friend*?" This was the first Gates had heard of someone on the outside possessing knowledge of the Clockstoppers project.

"Well . . . no, no, we can trust this dude," backpedaled Dopler. "I mean, he's outside, but he's cool. He's my old college professor, okay? If anybody can crack this math, it's him."

"Exactly *what* data did you send him?"

"Actually, um . . . I sent him a watch."

Gates closed his eyes and began methodically rubbing his temples. He had suffered from terrible migraines since his youth, but using a form of self-hypnosis, he'd mastered the ability to will them away. Only occasionally, in times of extreme stress, did he succumb to the blinding headaches. Right now was shaping up to be one of those times.

"Where exactly is that watch?" he uttered through clenched teeth. Gates massaged his temples harder, which accentuated the psychotic look in his eyes.

Dopler had let the cat out of the bag, he knew that, but it was too late to wrangle it back. Moreover, he had no doubt that his life was hanging by a thread. As much as he cared for Professor Gibbs and his family, he simply had no choice.

Dopler shivered, let out a fog-filled sigh, and gave Gates the address.

NINE

PLUR 102 was jammed with young bodies. Formerly a warehouse, the cavernous space had been transformed into party central, complete with motion lighting, halogen strobes and fog machines. It was dark, loud and colorful, the whole place pulsating to a techno trance groove.

A small stage at one end of the massive dance floor featured two mixing consoles with turntables. Between them stood a larger-than-life man in flowing robes, well known to the crowd as "Large Mike." A professional DJ and rapper of local renown, Large Mike was officiating the spin-off, which currently had two college-aged rave rats pitted against each other.

Meeker was in the audience, wearing psychedelic pants that might've looked good on Austin

Powers in 1968, but in the current millennium looked ridiculous. He tried to flow with the beat, but his nerves were tweaking him. Meeker was just about to go up against Dit-O, who was hangin' loose with Jocko on the other side of the stage. Dit-O's hip attire was on the money. Worse, he projected utter confidence.

Large Mike strutted behind the first college DJ as he mixed and scratched. The audience applaud-meter kicked in—the kid was smooth and had attitude. When he handed the mix over to his competitor—a serious slickster with cool dance moves and scratching par excellence—the glow-necklaced crowd *really* gave it up.

"The people have spoken," boomed Large Mike's voice over the P.A. "This round goes to . . . Flavius!"

Meeker tried to clap his sweaty hands. The loser of this round was *twice* the DJ he was—what was he thinking? He looked around for moral support in the form of Zak, but couldn't find his friend in the sea of faces, fog and lights. Zak had promised he would be there—what happened?

Zak *was* there, standing toward the back with Francesca. Both were absorbing the scene as Large Mike chanted into his cordless microphone.

"Now, let's keep the vibe going with our next two DJs—Dit-O on my right, and DJ Meeker comin' up on my left!"

Ditmar strutted onto the stage, cheered on by Jocko and a gaggle of slacker friends.

Meeker hesitated at the foot of the stairs. He thought seriously about slipping into the shadows before things got ugly, but that option vanished when the spotlight hit him. He shuddered, climbed the risers, and took his place behind the console.

"Let's go, boys!" bellowed Large Mike. "On your mix!"

Dit-O shot Meeker an intimidating leer to psyche him out, which easily worked. Meeker's nemesis immediately took charge and mixed a highly funkifized vinyl sample into a slick groove. He was good, and the crowd let him know it.

"Niiiiiice," praised Large Mike. "Okay, Meeker, it's comin' your way!"

Meeker nervously cued up his track and took over the mix. It didn't take a musical genius to realize his scratching was missing all the beats. Meeker tried to drown out his mistakes by boosting the bass, but it only muddied the mix and solicited some boos. Before it got any worse, he threw it back to Dit-O with relief.

Zak and Francesca painfully witnessed all of this. Seeing his best friend make a fool out of himself stunk, but even with the magic watch at his disposal, Zak didn't know how he could help.

Dit-O and company, however, were in heaven. Not only was he totally "on," but Dit-O was thoroughly humiliating Meeker the freaker. It just didn't get any better. Inspired by the landslide of support, Dit-O began to throw some decent dance moves into his routine. Jocko jumped onto the stage, egging on the crowd to give up more applause.

Meeker glanced across the stage, dreading the moment Dit-O would pass the mix back. As if sensing Meeker's anxiety, Dit-O threw it over with no warning. Meeker was lost as he slid the faders and spun the vinyl. It succeeded only in making undanceable noise. Dit-O and his throng began to laugh uncontrollably as the boos kicked in.

Meeker struggled on, but it was no use. He was going down in flames. Worse, he would be facing humiliation and torture from Dit-O and his crew for years to come.

I can deal with this, he rationalized. *I'll drop out of school, I'll change my name . . .*

"He's really not very smooth, is he?" Francesca's empathy wasn't reserved for Meeker alone. She could see what this was doing to Zak.

"I can't take it anymore," she blurted. Francesca grabbed Zak's wrist and activated the watch.

Suddenly the music was sucked into a sound vacuum, along with the voices of everyone in the club. The spinning lights, the fog and the crowd all froze. Not a creature was stirring, not even a DJ.

There were two exceptions, of course—Zak and Francesca. She cut a body-shaped tunnel through the fog as she made her way to the stage. Zak followed, stepping between the dancing bodies with their wildly frozen hair and clothes. He was definitely curious about what his Venezuelan date had planned.

Francesca walked around Meeker as if she were

examining an absurd sculpture. He had tried to salvage his feeble mixing with excruciatingly bad dance moves, one of which was now ludicrously captured in time.

"Help me move his feet," she asked as Zak joined her on the stage. Francesca leaned down and moved Meeker's foot a few inches.

"What are we doing?"

"A little dance lesson. Just move him a little bit at a time."

They began to move Meeker as if he were a clay figure—one arm up, the other down, twisting and turning him like a stop-motion character in a cartoon.

"It's just like playing with dolls," she laughed. "Let's lift him off the ground now."

She took one side of his body as Zak grabbed the other. Together they hoisted him and spun him around a few times. Zak was beginning to get into it.

"Wouldn't you love to see what this looks like?"

Although the two of them didn't get that privilege, the rest of the crowd certainly did. And what they saw changed their opinion of Meeker 180 degrees. He had been transformed into a dancing maniac, a groove god who pulled off moves that defied gravity. The *pièce de résistance* came when Meeker flipped upside down, balanced his head on the turntable and scratched out a happening groove with his scalp.

Large Mike just stood back and gaped as the audience went absolutely insane. There was a new sheriff in town, and his name was Meeker Smith.

At the other end of the stage, Dit-O and his entourage went slack-jaw. But the worst was yet to come for the would-be phat man.

Back in hypertime, Francesca had moved over to Dit-O. "Stop messing around and help me out over here," she called to Zak.

Zak lifted Meeker off the turntable and joined her. She was animating the spiky-haired Dit-O in ways reminiscent of very bad ballet.

"Now that's just wrong," grinned Zak as he admired her choreography.

"No, it's *Swan Lake*," she answered with a glint in her eye. Francesca had studied ballet extensively. Dit-O was now receiving the full benefit of her knowledge.

In real time, the crowd exploded into laughter. Dit-O had his fingers locked over his head as he launched into a very feminine pirouette. He then fluttered across the stage on his tiptoes with his neck cocked in a most dramatic pose. It was *Swan Lake* like no one had ever seen it.

The unfortunate Dit-O had no idea what was happening to him. He had zero control of his body, but that wasn't the worst part. He knew, beyond all doubt, that he would be the laughingstock of his peers for years to come.

"And I swear, I swear, I thought I was going to wet my pants!"

Meeker was cackling from the back of Francesca's

convertible as she drove the three of them home. Technically, the car belonged to her eldest brother, but he trusted her with it on special occasions. Tonight's date with Zak absolutely qualified.

"This hypertime thing is so trippy!" continued Meeker. "What are we going to do now, man? That watch is off the hook, baby!"

By now they had told him everything. Meeker gazed at the watch as if it were a winning lotto ticket worth zillions. Lots of ideas were dancing in his head.

"Hey, let's go dress Coach Wells up like Britney Spears!"

"I thought you were supposed to be home half an hour ago," said Zak. He gave Meeker a pointed look. He wanted to spend some time alone with his date and hoped Meeker would take the hint.

Meeker was clueless.

"Yo! Leslie Miller's having a slumber party tonight, and she's got that pool. . . . C'mon, they'll never see us!"

Francesca shot him a disapproving look, which also flew under Meeker's radar.

"No, Vegas . . . Vegas, baby! We could totally rack up, or maybe we could . . ."

"Hey, genius, we're not going anywhere," interrupted Zak. "My dad'll ground me for life if he finds out we've been messing with this thing."

Before Meeker could protest, Zak gestured for Francesca to pull over at the next house. It was a nice two-story brick home. *Meeker's* home.

Meeker's face sank. "Fine. I can take a hint."

He climbed out, thought twice, and hurried to Zak's side of the car.

"Sure you don't want me to come with you?"

Zak rolled the window up, Meeker's chin rising with it.

"Okay, okay!" He yanked his head back.

"Good night, Meeker."

"Have fun making out!" shouted Meeker as they pulled away, loud enough so all the neighbors could hear it.

A fraction of a second later, his pants magically dropped down around his ankles.

"Okay, that's it—you're abusing your powers!" he whined, fumbling his pants back up. "I'm telling the Super Friends!"

A quarter of an hour later, Francesca was pulling into her own driveway. She turned off the convertible's engine, allowing the chirping of crickets to fill the void. She and Zak had shared a once-in-a-lifetime experience, no question. What they shared now was nervous excitement. Their mutual attraction was obvious.

Francesca spoke first.

"So . . ."

"So . . ." he echoed.

They both smiled awkwardly.

"So this has turned out not so bad after all, Mr. Second Chance Man."

Zak nodded, giving it some thought. "See, the way I figure it, if you make a really bad first impression, things can only get better."

Francesca grinned back. She glanced at Zak's watch, which simply displayed the time now. "Oh, I better go."

"Now?" Zak did not want this night to end. Ever.

"Yes . . . at midnight, my father blinks the porch light, and I turn back into a pumpkin."

Zak peered at the watch. It was 23:59. One minute till midnight.

"Oh, wow. I gotta go too."

His eyebrows rose with a thought.

"Then again, midnight could be a long time off."

He reached for the button, but she stopped him.

"You think that magic watch is going to get you a kiss?"

"No," he said quickly. "I was just, you know, hoping we could spend some more time togeth—"

"Shh. You don't need magic."

Francesca leaned closer and gave him a sweet, tender kiss. Although it lasted maybe three seconds, it was imprinted in his memory forever.

"Sweet dreams, Mr. Second Chance Man. It was fun."

She climbed from the car and went inside.

Zak sat in the passenger seat for a full minute, appreciating the wisp of perfume she had left behind. Injected with a new lease on life, he sprang from the convertible without opening the door and hopped on his bike.

In record time, Zak was speeding through a frozen downtown on his way home. He had decided to make the journey in hypertime, though he really didn't need the exhilaration. In his current state of mind, he had the energy of ten men.

He would soon need it.

As Zak pulled into his driveway, he saw several flashlights whipping around inside his darkened home. This could mean only one thing: he was not alone in hypertime.

TEN

Rubber-gloved hands were rifling through wooden drawers and loose electronics down in Professor Gibbs's basement workshop. The hands belonged to Jay, who was in search of the watch and any research pertaining to it. She had a weapon slung over her shoulder with an attached gas canister. Jay slammed a drawer shut and flung a stack of lecture notes piled on the workbench. As soon as the papers left her grip, they eerily froze in the air.

One flight above, Henry Gates impatiently waited as Richard and a subordinate QT agent tore apart Zak's room. Richard came across a small, framed snapshot of Zak and his father in happier times. He tossed it to Gates, then spotted the professor's itinerary and hotel information amidst Zak's models. He slipped it into his inside coat pocket.

They didn't know that Zak and their precious watch were right outside, stealthily moving to the back door. Zak spotted his baseball bat on the porch and grabbed it as an afterthought. He carefully slid his house key into the deadbolt and opened the door. *I'm either being really brave or really stupid*, he thought. He reminded himself that his mother and sister were inside, gathered up his courage, and crept in.

Zak was relieved to find Mom and Kelly on the den couch eating popcorn, bonding over a TV special on boy bands. A kernel of popcorn floated a few inches in front of Kelly's open mouth. The image on TV, like the rest of the world, was also rendered motionless.

Zak heard noise beneath him. He carefully widened the basement door and furtively descended the wooden stairs. Halfway down, he glimpsed Jay tearing apart his dad's workbench. She was facing away from him, which gave him a full view of her futuristic-looking weapon.

Zak swallowed hard and readied his Louisville slugger.

Then, just above him, the rickety stairs creaked.

Zak hazarded a glance backwards. A pair of legs belonging to another QT agent was coming into view. Zak rapidly turned and whacked him hard in the knees.

Jay instantly spun around, leveled her weapon, and blasted a white icy cloud at Zak. He didn't know what it was, nor did he wait around to find out. Scrambling past the goon he'd downed, Zak dodged the burst of liquid nitrogen, which hit the agent instead. The guy barely had time to holler as he was painfully jolted back into real time, freezing on the staircase.

Gates and Richard heard the commotion, but by now Zak was rocketing out the back door. As he sprinted across the lawn, Zak decided that entering his house had been really brave *and* really stupid. He ran onto the street and ducked behind a white van, stopping to catch his breath and strategize.

At first he didn't see the small QT logo on the van's door. By the time he did, the door was sliding open and a hand was yanking him inside.

Zak elbow-jabbed and head-butted his captor as he struggled in the darkness.

"Shhhh! Oww! Shut up, dang it, hold still, man!" One of the man's wrists was cuffed to an armrest.

"Who are you?" shouted Zak. "What do you people want?"

Having aged over twenty years in the last two days, Earl Dopler wasn't easy for Zak to recognize, especially in the low light.

"Uh . . . they want to kill you, man." Dopler gestured through the windshield at Zak's house. Gates, Richard, Jay and two other QT agents were on the porch, trying to assess where Zak might've gone.

"Why?" asked Zak, his voice quieter but no less agitated. "What did I do?"

"You showed up, and you're running around with something that isn't supposed to exist. Now get in the driver's seat!"

Zak had no time to question the directive. He hopped behind the wheel and reached for the ignition.

More bad news.

"There're no keys!"

"Grab the wires under the dash," Dopler instructed.

Zak reached beneath the steering wheel and pulled out a tangle of wires.

"Excellent," said the scientist. "Now bite the green one."

Zak obeyed . . . and instantaneously received twelve volts from a car battery that nearly fried his lips.

"Aaaaaagghhh!!!"

"Okay, that's not the one," shrugged Dopler.

Zak just glared back, his mouth still sizzling.

"Strip the *red* wire with your teeth and touch it to the steering column," Dopler revised.

Zak didn't move. He wasn't about to suffer this fool a second time.

"Hurry, man—they're coming!"

Dopler was right. Two of Gates's men were making their way toward the van, their jackets bulging with weapons.

Zak squeezed his eyes shut and cautiously bit into the wire.

No shock.

He stripped it with his incisors and touched it to the metal.

VROOOM.

"He's in the van!" shouted one of the agents as the engine roared to life. By the time they had their weapons drawn, the van was speeding off.

Gates strolled down the front lawn and watched his van screech around a corner.

"Go after them," he calmly ordered Richard and Jay. His marathon headache was finally beginning to subside.

His lackeys dashed to their silver sedan and immediately gave chase.

Fifty yards ahead, Zak was racing onto the main boulevard that led into downtown. He immediately had to swerve—an SUV sat motionless in the intersection, its headlight beams bizarrely split like colorful prisms. Zak and Dopler were moving fast enough to witness the outer edges of the actual speed of light.

"Aw, man! You're going to get us killed!" screamed Dopler as Zak barely avoided the SUV.

"Hey, this is harder than it looks!" Zak yelled back. Just as he cleared the intersection, they found a huge delivery truck staring back at them.

"AAAAAHHHHH!"

Both of them shrieked as Zak jerked the wheel and plowed into a newspaper stand on the sidewalk. Papers and wood splinters went flying, eerily freezing in the air as soon as they cleared the van.

Swerving back onto the road, Zak felt a

deepening dread as he caught a glimpse of the sedan in his side mirror. It was mowing down landscaping on the opposite sidewalk and catching up quick.

"Who are those guys?" Zak asked with a swallow. One thing he knew for sure—these were no ordinary burglars.

"You don't want to know, man."

Dopler was right again. Zak didn't want to know. But it was too late to stick his head in the sand.

"What were they shooting at me?"

"Liquid nitrogen, man," explained the scientist. "It's a quick and dirty come-down from hypertime. The cold slows your molecular activity." Dopler's eyeballs rolled down to Zak's wrist, which had a watch-sized lump beneath his sweat-jacket sleeve. "Now, exactly what are you doing with the watch?"

Zak dropped his arm out of view. He wasn't ready to give it up, at least not to this guy. "What watch?"

"*What watch?*" mimicked Dopler. "Dude, I'm *not* the security guard at K-Mart."

Zak avoided a response by swerving around another car. Dopler glared at Zak in the rearview. He'd deal with the kid later. Right now he needed to get free. Dopler leaned forward and fished inside the glove box. He came up with a tiny screwdriver.

"Probably faster to just gnaw my hand off," he muttered as he slipped the tool into his cuffs and attempted to pick the lock.

BAM!

The sedan had caught up and was ramming the van's rear bumper.

"Are they trying to kill you, too, or is it just me?" uttered Zak.

BAM!

"Oh, I'd say they're probably up for a two-fer at this point," replied Dopler, not the speediest lockpick in the world.

Richard floored the gas pedal of the sedan and swerved to the left side of the van. Zak risked a glance and saw Jay smiling back at him from the passenger side.

WHAM!

They slammed into the van's side. They were trying to force Zak onto the shoulder. Dopler took the hint and redoubled his lock-picking efforts.

WHAM!

Zak couldn't get off the shoulder. Worse, huge concrete pilings were blocking his path ahead.

"Hang on!" screamed Zak.

He spun the wheel and rammed the side of the sedan as hard as he could. It was a kamikaze maneuver, no question, but it succeeded in temporarily subduing the bad guys. The demolition derby inspired Dopler to focus all his concentration on the lock. If he didn't get free soon, he was gonna die.

Click.

The handcuffs sprung free. He hopped into the passenger seat and immediately lunged for Zak's wrist.

"Give me the watch!"

"No way!" shouted Zak, nearly losing control

of the van as they struggled. "Without the watch, I'm just a big frozen target!"

"Not my problem, man. Now hand it over!"

Dopler raised the tiny screwdriver like a weapon. Zak gazed at it.

"Or what? You're gonna *adjust* me to death?"

BAM!

Richard and Jay were back, madder than ever. Both vehicles were now traversing a narrow bridge, barely wide enough for two cars. They rammed the van's rear with a vengeance as Dopler and Zak fought over the watch.

BAM!

The sedan rammed the van just as Dopler yanked Zak's wrist. In the process, the left bezel button got pushed.

Hypertime abruptly ended.

The molecular deceleration passed through the van and shot Zak and Dopler back into real time. Much to their fortune, the sedan had been touching the van's bumper just as the watch had been deactivated. *Both* vehicles had been taken into real time.

HONNNNNKKKK!

A huge moving van was thundering across the bridge from the opposite direction.

"AAAAAHHHHH!"

Zak and Dopler were shrieking in harmony again. They had a choice between a head-on collision, or going over the edge.

SMASH!

The van careened through the guardrail. What awaited Zak and Dopler beyond the railing saved their lives.

SPLASH!

The van swan-dived into a river below, which cushioned their fall. Still, the impact was hard enough to toss Dopler out the door and render Zak unconscious behind the wheel.

Dopler surfaced and spit out the murky water. The van was floating upright about thirty feet away, with Zak half-hanging out of his sprung door.

"You gotta give me the watch, man!"

Zak had no reaction as Dopler started to drift downstream. Within ten seconds he lost sight of Zak, and was too weak to swim back. Dopler called out a final time—

"Whatever you do, don't get it wet, man!"

Zak stirred, his arm flopping out the door.

His wrist hit the water with a small splash.

ELEVEN

The big fly lumbered across the emergency room, its wings barely flapping enough to keep it aloft. It landed on the wall clock, its second hand struggling to tick forward. Doctors and nurses performed their duties in bizarre slow motion, their shouted orders sounding like a tape recorder with the batteries dying.

It all seemed like a bad dream to Zak, who felt like he'd been hit by a truck . . . or in his case, a large body of water.

Dr. Juarez leaned over him. She was in her forties and had friendly eyes.

"Soooooo . . . ssstrange . . . seeems . . . fine . . . but . . . his . . . vitals . . . are . . . doubled. . . ."

Her voice was low and slurred, but seemed to be speeding up.

The watch was still tightly strapped to Zak's wrist, but it was far from functional. Its face was clouded with condensation and the display was behaving strangely. Tiny arcs of electricity danced and sparked under the crystal as the digital numbers scrolled somewhere between real time and hypertime. The frenetic energy inside the watch continued to build until there was a bright flash. The display went dark.

At the exact same moment, the E.R. and its inhabitants resumed to normal speed.

"Here he comes," smiled the doctor. "Good morning, Sleeping Beauty."

Struggling for coherence, Zak hadn't noticed the tall thin man in the tired brown suit who had been hovering nearby. The man pushed his way past the doctor to Zak's bedside.

"Where'd you get the van, kid?"

His badge identified him as Detective Freemont, and nobody ever used the word "pleasant" to describe him.

"Not now, Detective," admonished Dr. Juarez. "Let him breathe."

"Is he okay?" asked Zak's mom as she rushed into the room. She and his sister, Kelly, had just arrived at the hospital.

"He'll be all right. It's just a mild concussion," Dr. Juarez reassured. Mrs. Gibbs stroked her son's forehead as if he was still in kindergarten.

"Hey baby, how you feeling?"

"Uh . . . I'm fine, I think," uttered Zak, little more than half awake.

"Good, so you can stand trial," Kelly piped up, looking for attention.

"What?" he mumbled back.

"Hello?! You stole a van and crashed it!" she said with a certain amount of glee. "Mom, can I have Zak's room while he's in jail? Please, please . . ."

Detective Freemont was losing what little patience he had. He wedged himself between Mrs. Gibbs and the doctor.

"You almost got yourself killed with that little joyriding stunt, son," he started in.

"I don't know what got into him," defended Zak's mother. "He's a really good kid, *really*."

Zak watched them as if he were detached from his body. He was coherent enough to realize that the gruff cop meant serious business, but trouble with the police was the least of his worries. He was in first-class danger. He had to tell them about the watch, about everything. Zak labored to make the words spinning in his head come out of his mouth.

"No, you don't understand," he began shakily. "We were in hypertime . . . they were after my watch . . . it's a molecular accelerator." Zak reached for the watch and punched several buttons, all to no avail.

"Oh no, they're gonna kill me!" He was now sitting upright and fully caffeinated with fear.

"Who's going to kill you?" the detective jumped in.

"Those people . . . who were in our house . . . you can't see them 'cause they're invisible," Zak said with conviction.

Freemont's brow crumpled.

"Uh-huh."

He made some notes on his pad, including the word "liar." As the detective pondered how to proceed, a gawky young street cop delivered him a cup of coffee. The rookie's hat was two sizes too big and squashed down his ears, giving him a dopey look. Detective Freemont looked down into the contents of the paper cup and made a face like it was old motor oil.

"I said creamer, you twit," he snapped.

Zak quickly came to the realization that these police officers were going to be of no help. "I can't stay here," he said to no one in particular, then scrambled to get out of bed. Dr. Juarez tried to hold Zak down for his own protection, but the teenager had a full tank of adrenaline.

"Nurse!"

Zak rushed to the window and confirmed his suspicions: A sleek sedan with lots of dents had just pulled up outside. The man and woman who'd been chasing him earlier climbed out and entered the hospital.

"They're gonna kill me!" he shouted again, looking positively freaked.

Zak's mom stood by helplessly as a pair of orderlies struggled to contain him. Dr. Juarez approached Zak with a syringe full of high-octane sedative.

"No! No!" the teen screamed.

"He is *so* fakin' it," giggled Kelly, who was busy playing with the controls on Zak's bed.

Zak got one look at the big needle coming his way and decided it was time for Plan B.

"Uh, you know what, I *am* faking it," he blurted out, no longer struggling. "I'm really sorry I stole the van . . . and I'd love to tell you about it."

His declaration kept the needle at bay. Pen and pad prepped, Detective Freemont leaned in to hear Zak's confession.

"I gotta pee," he said sheepishly. "And as soon as I'm done, I'll tell you all about it."

Zak dashed inside the bathroom before the detective could protest. His only hope was to get the watch working and get out of there quick. Zak unstrapped it, shook it, and blotted it with his hospital gown.

The watch remained nonfunctional.

He then spotted his final chance—mounted on the bathroom wall was a hot-air hand dryer. Zak smacked the ON button and desperately waved the watch under the noisy blower.

"Come on, come on . . ."

Just outside, the detective heard the noise and got suspicious.

"What are you doing in there?" he demanded.

"I can't go unless there's some noise," Zak called back.

Freemont shot a glance at Mrs. Gibbs. She confirmed this fact with an awkward nod.

Inside, Zak desperately continued to frantically dry the watch. He felt a huge surge of hope when he noticed the watch display flickering back to life. The hand dryer was working!

Bang-bang-bang.

Freemont was pounding on the door.

"Let's go!" bellowed the detective. "Time's up!"

Zak strapped on the watch and crossed his fingers.

Outside the E.R., doctors, nurses and patients suddenly froze in motion.

Richard and Jay strolled through the doors and marched past the real-life mannequins; Gates's lackeys were unmistakably in hypertime. They made their way around the living statues, passing by the gawky street cop. The rookie's head was down, his face obscured by his oversized hat. In his hand was a cup of coffee, with cream.

If Richard and Jay had been paying more attention, they would have noticed that the young cop wasn't wearing any shoes. Disguised in the rookie's uniform, Zak concentrated with all his being to keep perfectly still. The watch had indeed worked—he was also in hypertime. The question was *how long* it would last, as the device appeared to be shorting out again.

Richard and Jay continued down the hall and glanced inside the E.R.

"*Go in, go in,*" Zak quietly chanted.

They did.

The second they were out of view, Zak took off down the hall.

Inside Zak's hospital room, Richard and Jay recognized Zak's mom waiting outside the bathroom door, so it didn't take Sherlock Holmes to deduce who was inside. They swung the door open and spotted "Zak" standing at the toilet. They spun him around, only to discover the rookie cop dressed in Zak's hospital gown.

By now, Zak was sprinting full tilt out of the hospital. He dashed in front of a paramedic van just as the watch began to spark and fizzle. There was a small, bright flash, and—*pfft*—the watch died.

Zak crashed into real time as the hospital environs sprang back to life. He frantically tapped on the watch crystal, keenly aware that Richard and Jay remained dangerously close, and that he was a very, very slow moving target.

Henry Gates stood on the main floor of the research room at QT Labs, peering at the ion stabilizer. It was nearly identical to the computer-generated image he'd seen on Dopler's monitor in the Clean Room—a reclining seat housed in a cage full of electronics. The problem was that it wasn't operational.

Gates held a framed photo of Zak and his dad, the one acquired by Richard during their "visit" at the Gibbs residence. Gates's other hand gripped a cell phone pressed firmly to his ear. It was evident from his flushed face that he was not happy with what he was hearing.

"You two can save me your lame excuses and just get back here," he fumed as he smashed the picture frame against the stabilizer housing. It wasn't an impulsive move—Gates ripped the snapshot from its frame and tore it down the middle, sliding the half with Zak's image into a large manila envelope.

"I've got something I want delivered to our contact at the FBI," he resumed.

Gates walked to a printer and grabbed a grainy black-and-white photo of Dopler that had been captured from video security footage.

"A little publicity ought to flush out Dopler and the kid. After all, we can't kill what we can't find."

Richard and Jay were conversing with Gates over the speakerphone inside the sedan. They traded a glance, trying to figure out their boss's logic.

"But without Dopler, how do we finish the ion stabilizer?" asked Richard.

Gates looked at the remaining half of the photo in his hand . . . at the smiling face of Professor George Gibbs.

"Open your mind, Richard. Who needs the student, when the teacher's so close at hand?"

TWELVE

"**H**i, Eryka. . . . Good to see you, Helga. . . ."

Meeker stood behind the counter at X-Dream Sports. He was thumbing through a magazine, imagining that the pictured models would actually give him the time of day.

The ringing phone snapped him out of his delusion.

"X-Dream Sports, Junior Associate Manager Meeker speaking . . ."

"I need your mom's car," said the voice on the other end.

"Zak? Dude! What's going on? I heard the cops are looking for you."

"Turn around slowly," said Zak. "But be cool, you don't want to be seen with me."

Meeker swiveled and looked out the front door.

Zak was standing at a pay phone across the street, discreetly waving a nightstick in Meeker's direction. He was still dressed in the rookie's uniform.

"I need you to go home and get the keys to your mom's Subaru."

"Are you crazy?" answered Meeker too loudly.

"Somebody's trying to kill me over this watch!" countered Zak, trying not to raise his own voice.

"Then you don't need a Subaru! You need the police!"

Zak lowered the phone and stepped into full view. He glared at Meeker, as if to say: *Look what I'm wearing, you idiot.* Zak grabbed the receiver again.

"I just came from the police. They weren't as helpful as you'd think."

"Oh," he lamely replied.

"I gotta get to Kingston to see my dad. Maybe he can figure out how to call these people off."

"Dude, that's like a six-hour drive!"

"*Dude*, I'm kind of desperate here!"

"Why don't you call him?"

"I did that already! I can't get ahold of him!"

Zak was losing his patience. He started to march across the street when something grabbed his attention. Detective Freemont and a uniformed officer were flat-footing it down the sidewalk in his direction.

Zak quickly ducked behind the booth as they jay-walked into X-Dream Sports. He figured they were there to question Meeker since they were friends.

"I gotta go!" he blurted, "and you don't know anything, understand?" Zak quickly hung up, turned to run, and found himself face-to-face with a pair of octogenarians who were gawking at his bare feet. Zak tipped his police hat and feigned a smile.

"Budget cuts."

He sidestepped the elderly couple and jogged off.

The moon was just coming up over the red tile roof of Francesca's home. Incandescent lights and laughter leaked from the hacienda's arched windows.

The occupants had no idea that someone was creeping around outside. The intruder snuck to the window, peered through it, and saw a dozen people congregating in the formal dining room. Francesca's parents were entertaining family and friends. Francesca was sipping coffee beside her father, a jovial-faced man who was telling a story that made everyone at the table chuckle.

The intruder was Zak. Still in the stolen uniform and wanted by the police, he thought it unwise to barge in and explain his predicament to Francesca's parents and their guests. Besides, he wasn't sure he *could* explain it.

Zak spotted a trellis on the side of the house, which rose to an upstairs window. He grabbed it and began to climb.

Francesca's room was filled with family photos and posters from all the places she'd traveled. Tired after the party, Francesca entered her room and started to undress for bed. She glanced at herself in the vanity mirror over her dresser.

There was a note taped to it:

FRANCESCA—I need your help. Don't be afraid, I'm in your room.

ZAK

She quickly buttoned her blouse and spun around. The room appeared to be empty, but Francesca suspected otherwise. She waved her hands around as if she were trying to touch a ghost.

"Okay, Mr. Invisible, where are you?"

She heard her bathroom toilet flush. A moment later, "Officer Zak" stepped out. Before he could explain—

"You broke into my house just to pee?"

He started to answer but was cut off again.

"*What* are you wearing?"

Zak had rehearsed his explanation for maximum credibility, but decided it made no sense no matter how he served it up. He reverted to the Cliff's Notes version, his words delivered like machine-gun fire:

"Listen, I know this is weird and it's the last thing you want to hear from a guy after only one date but the cops are looking for me everywhere and I've got nowhere else to go—I just need some clothes and money for the bus. I promise I'll pay you back."

Francesca just stared.

"O*kay*. What's going on, Zak?"

"It's a long story and the less you know the better," he said at a slightly slower speed. "I just . . . things with this watch have gotten really twisted and I need to get to Kingston to find my dad, and . . ."

A sudden thought hit him brick-hard.

"Oh my God, they could be after him too!"

"Whoa, whoa!" she interrupted. "*Who's* after you? What are you talking about?"

"I don't know," he honestly answered. "I have no clue who they are, and—and—"

Zak started to crack. He had been making up his strategy minute by minute, and the current sixty seconds were overloading his circuits.

"I'm sorry. I shouldn't have come," he mumbled. Zak started to climb back out the window. She stopped him.

"Shhh. Come here . . ."

Francesca took his hand and made him sit down on her bed.

"I'm glad you came," she softly said. "But if we're going to be friends, you have to tell me what's happening."

Zak took a breath and began to go over what little he knew.

Ten minutes later, they were walking across her circular driveway. Her brother's convertible was parked outside the garage.

"Listen, I told my brother I was getting it

detailed, so bring it back clean." She tried to smile as she handed him the keys. Zak faced her with a look that revealed more than just gratitude.

"I can't thank you enough."

"Call me when you find your dad?"

Zak nodded. She stepped closer and hugged him. He found it difficult to let go, and so did she. He eventually climbed behind the wheel.

Francesca watched him with mixed feelings as he started up the car. Having shared the power of the watch with him, she felt they were in this together. More than that, she silently admitted to herself that she actually might be falling for him.

Francesca impulsively climbed into the passenger seat. Zak shot her a look.

"What are you doing?"

"You raked my leaves. . . . I can't let you go alone."

She was trying to be glib, but he could read between the lines. She genuinely cared about him. But Zak didn't want to get her involved more than she already was. He'd likely be risking his life and didn't want to risk hers.

The decision, however, wasn't his to make. When he started to object, her look was firm: *If you want to take this car, I'm going.*

He began to rationalize. She was very intelligent, and resourceful. He definitely could use the help.

Truth be told, Zak was thrilled that Francesca was joining him.

* * *

"I feel like such an idiot," Professor Gibbs said into the hotel room phone. "He was calling all day . . ."

Gibbs was cradling the receiver in the crook of his neck as he hurriedly packed his suitcase. By now his wife had brought him up to speed. Zak had stolen a van and had gone on a joyride. Zak was wanted by the police. Now Zak was missing.

"I kept meaning to check my messages," he muttered guiltily. "I never should've gone off with things like this between us."

Professor Gibbs knew that he'd left his son upset, but he honestly couldn't believe these accusations. Zak was a good kid. Zak was smart. There had to be an explanation.

"George, George, listen—calm down," his wife told him. She was having a hard time practicing what she preached as she paced around her living room. She'd been up all night keeping a vigil and had dark circles under her eyes.

It didn't help that Detective Freemont was perched on the couch like a vulture, constantly jotting into his notepad.

"The police want you to stay there in case Zak calls again," she relayed.

The detective hopped off his perch and swooped closer.

"He giving you trouble? Because I can talk to him," said Freemont with authority. Mrs. Gibbs waved him off.

"Believe me, George, if he shows up here, I'll let you know."

"Fine," Gibbs said with frustration. "I just feel so helpless sitting here waiting."

"Welcome to the club," she tersely replied. Stress and lack of sleep had definitely taken their toll. "I'm sorry, I didn't mean it like that," she apologized. "It's just . . . I've been everywhere trying to track him down, and we couldn't reach you, and . . ."

"All right, all right . . . let's go over your list of places again," said her husband, forcing a calm voice.

Three floors down, a man in a plain blue shirt and baseball cap had just entered the Kingston Hotel lobby through a side door. Dopler pulled his cap a little lower, doing his best to be inconspicuous as he approached the front desk.

"Yeah, I, uh, need the room number for Dr. George Gibbs," he told the middle-aged woman with GUEST RELATIONS clipped to her burgundy blazer. "He's here with the convention."

She looked Dopler up and down as if the sight of him produced intestinal gas.

"And you are . . . ?"

"In a hurry."

Dopler slid a crumpled hundred-dollar bill across the counter. She briefly eyed it, then met his intense gaze.

"I'm not supposed to give out room numbers, sir."

He sensed the latitude in her voice and slid another hundred her way. She strained a smile.

"But occasionally we can make an exception," she added as she took the cash and moved to the hotel computer.

Upstairs, Professor Gibbs was still on the phone with his wife. Resolving to stay put, he had switched from packing to pacing.

"Did he say anything else that might explain his behavior?"

Mrs. Gibbs tried to think. "Not really. He rambled a little when he first came to . . . let me see . . ." She moved to her purse, pulling out a small pad she kept for grocery lists and self-reminders. She had jotted down what Zak had said in the E.R.

"Here it is," she offered, finding the right page. "He said something about his watch being a molecular accelerator or something . . ."

Professor Gibbs sunk to the bed. "Molecular accelerator? Oh no . . . "

His mind raced. *Did Zak find the watch? Did he launch himself into hypertime?*

"Jenny, listen. I need you to go downstairs and look on the shelf above my workbench. There should be a box with a watch in it. See if it's still there."

"What's going on, George?"

"I'll tell you in a minute," he answered tensely. "Just check the box."

Mrs. Gibbs set down the receiver and hurried off. Detective Freemont narrowed his eyes and jotted more notes.

The professor glanced at his room TV. He had turned on the news to keep him company, but now he stared right through the screen. His concern for Zak had just tripled.

The knock at his door injected him with hope. "Zak?"

He dashed over and swung it open.

Henry Gates smiled back at him, flanked by Richard.

"Dr. Gibbs?"

The professor's face sank with disappointment. "Yes?"

"Henry Gates, QT Laboratories," he smiled, not offering his hand. "I believe we have a mutual friend, Earl Dopler?"

Down the hall, the elevator door opened and Dopler stepped out. He snatched one look at the backside of Gates and did a quick about-face. Nobody saw him.

"Dr. Dopler tells us you're quite the expert on . . ."

"Look, whatever this is, it'll have to wait," Gibbs said impatiently. "I'm in the middle of something very important."

Gates pressed a button on his watch and Professor Gibbs froze, along with the rest of the world.

"Yes, you certainly are," smiled Gates.

THIRTEEN

"George? George?"

Mrs. Gibbs's tinny voice leaked from the beige phone receiver, which was dangling off the hotel nightstand.

No one answered.

Zak and Francesca pulled up outside the hotel. It had been a six-hour, all-night drive. She was leaning against his shoulder, fast asleep in the passenger seat as Zak turned into the alley across the street from the Kingston.

He eyed the building from a safe distance. It was not yet 5 A.M. and the hotel looked as asleep as Francesca. Zak gently squeezed her shoulder.

"Hey kiddo . . . Francesca?"

She stirred, her voice groggy.

"Are we there?"

"Yeah."

Zak took an apprehensive glance across the street, then opened his door. She stopped him, her voice still sleepy.

"Hold on. These hypertime guys, they're looking for you, right? Maybe I should go."

Even half-asleep, this girl was smart.

"You don't mind?"

"I don't usually like to meet a boy's father this soon, but, for you . . ."

She gave him a light kiss, confirming why she had really come along.

"Hey . . . while you're up there, could you tell him that taking the watch was your idea?"

Francesca smiled back as she opened the door.

"For you? No problem.".

Zak had a pang of fear as she climbed from the car, crossed the alley, and disappeared into the hotel. If anything happened to her, it would kill him.

He waited for what seemed like an eternity but was actually about five minutes. Zak audibly sighed when he saw Francesca exit the lobby doors and cross the street toward him.

"He didn't answer his phone and I found *this* on the door," she told him upon arrival, holding up a DO NOT DISTURB sign.

"Perfect," he muttered, growing concerned again. He thought for a moment.

"Let's go disturb."

They jogged across the street and entered through the hotel's side door, just as Dopler had done earlier. They avoided the lobby, stepped into the stairwell and scaled the three flights to his father's floor.

Zak slowly cracked the access door and spied the hallway. It was empty, but knowing there could be invisible antagonists waiting for them made his forehead sweat. He and Francesca took the plunge and moved to Room 312. He gently tried the knob.

Locked.

Zak knocked three times. Ten seconds passed with no response.

"Do you have a credit card?"

Francesca handed him one. He slid it into the jamb and jiggled it around. In a matter of moments the door clicked open. She gave him a look as he returned her card. He seemed to know an awful lot about breaking and entering.

"My dad taught me," he attempted to explain. "I mean, the mechanics are really simple . . ."

"I'm beginning to think you are a bad influence," she interjected with a small grin.

Zak eased the door open and they cautiously entered. The bed was disheveled. The phone was still off the hook. The news still blared on the room's TV. Stranger still, there was no luggage to be seen, nor clothes inside the mirrored closet.

Zak lifted the phone receiver and heard nothing. The phone had been off the hook for at least several minutes.

At the same time, Francesca approached the bathroom. Light leaked from beneath the closed door. She grabbed the knob and swung it open. It, too, was empty. All traces of Professor George Gibbs had been removed from the room.

She and Zak swapped perplexed looks. His gaze fell on the phone again. Zak hung up to get a dial tone and pressed the speed-dial button for the front desk.

"Good evening," said the slight, balding night manager as he squinted at the switchboard monitor. "How may I help you, Dr. Gibbs?"

Doctor Gibbs. Zak cleared his throat and deepened his voice.

"Um, have I checked out yet?"

"Not that I know of, sir."

"Did I change rooms?"

The night manager didn't hesitate. Working the graveyard shift, he was used to all kinds of wacky calls.

"No, sir, I don't believe you did."

Before Zak could conjure another question, Francesca grabbed his arm.

"Zak?"

She was watching the news. The QT Laboratories van was being fished out of the river.

"Dr. Gibbs?" asked the night manager, still on the line. "Is everything all right?"

Zak hung up without answering. He grabbed the remote and raised the volume:

"It seemed like a simple joyride in a stolen van,

until the FBI linked the teenage suspect to the theft of top-secret government research by this man, Dr. Earl Dopler . . ."

The black-and-white photo of Dopler, courtesy of Gates, filled the screen. The degenerated image made him look even older.

"That's not Dopler," said Zak. "Dopler was one of my dad's students, he's like twenty-eight. No way that guy is him . . ."

"Dr. Dopler is considered armed and extremely dangerous," resumed the newscaster.

"At least they didn't mention your name," said Francesca, trying to be positive.

"If you should see Dopler or Zak Gibbs, his teenaged accomplice, please contact your local FBI. . . ."

Zak's face splashed across the TV, larger than life.

"Okay. This is now officially freaking me out."

Zak jabbed the remote and extinguished the broadcast. He impulsively marched out of the room and retraced his steps down through the stairwell, a worried Francesca following him.

"Why don't we call my dad?" she suggested. "He knows people from the consulate. He can help."

"No," Zak fired back, "I'm not putting your family at risk." He arrived on the ground floor and shoved his way out the side door. "It's bad enough I got *you* involved."

"Hey, *macho muchacho—I* got me involved," she retorted. "But I should call just to let them know I'm okay."

He nodded, calming down a bit as they walked down the alley toward their car.

Beeeep—beeeep—beeeep . . .

A city trash truck was backing toward the bins in the alley, which were resting on the other side of the convertible. Whoever was driving was rolling straight for the car.

"What's this bozo up to?" said Zak.

The truck began to pick up speed.

"Stop!" he yelled, waving his hands.

"You're going to hit my brother's car!" screamed Francesca.

The truck kept moving backwards. It took up most of the alley and forced the teenagers onto a narrow sidewalk.

"Stop the truck!" Zak shouted a final time.

Before they realized what was happening, the truck's grabber arm snapped out and seized them.

"Hey!"

"What is happening?" screamed Francesca, justifiably terrified.

The answer came a heartbeat later when they felt their feet jerked off the pavement.

The grabber arm rose high into the air with Zak and Francesca in its claws. Before they could wriggle free, it pivoted and tossed them into the bowels of the truck.

FOURTEEN

Zak fell headfirst into the disgusting load of spoiled food and other smelly unmentionables. Francesca got off a bit easier, her drop cushioned by Zak as she landed on top of him.

"Are you all right . . . ?" he moaned. His words were hard to understand because his face was buried in a stained, shredded pillow leaking feathers.

Francesca rolled off of him, slipping between something slimy and something that squished.

"You know, the first date was nice. This one . . . not so much."

Trash piled above them began to cascade down as the truck lurched forward. Now buried up to his neck, Zak fished around and latched on to Francesca, who was completely submerged. Together they clawed their way above the muck just as the truck came to another jolting stop. The engine turned off, shuddered for a few seconds, and then went silent.

Footsteps could be heard moving to the rear of the truck.

"What's that?" she whispered, trying not to breathe in the stench.

"I don't know . . . just stay cool."

A blade of light sliced across them as the rear hatch opened with a metallic grind. A familiar pair of eyes squinted in at them.

"Hey, man. You ready to give me that watch?"

Dopler shoved the hatch open further, revealing a smug smile that said: *Am I clever or what?*

WHACK!

Francesca wiped away his grin with the heel of her foot. The kick sent Dopler reeling backwards with a bloody nose. He regained his balance and staggered back to the hatch.

"You know what I don't like, man? Getting kicked in the head! That is sub-par!"

Dopler slammed the hatch shut and threw them into darkness again.

"I didn't know you knew karate," said Zak, impressed.

"I don't. That was ballet."

Zak flashed on Dit-O's *Swan Lake* choreography. This girl was multitalented, no question about it.

The engine chugged to life and they began to

roll. Five minutes and five hundred rancid odors later, they halted again.

What's he gonna do now? wondered Zak.

Dopler answered by yanking all sorts of levers in the truck cab. Suddenly the floor was tilting under their feet. There was nothing to cling to as they felt themselves sliding.

WHOOSH!

The rear of the truck opened its jowls and spit out a sea of trash. Zak and Francesca were flopping in it like fish tossed on dry land. They got to their feet just in time to face Dopler, who appeared to be holding a weapon in his coat pocket.

"All right, little dude, hand it over, man," he said menacingly. "And don't even *think* about touching that dial!"

Zak knew the watch no longer functioned. Dopler, however, had no idea.

"Not until you tell me what you did with my dad," he countered. "I know you're a spy—it's all over the news!"

"They're lying, man! I love my country! Now give me the watch so I can go to Costa Rica. I really, really, *really* need a vacation." Dopler swiveled and aimed his gun, or rather pocket, at Francesca. "And no funny stuff or your hottie gets it."

"Okay . . . okay," Zak said quickly. He was not willing to call the man's bluff, not with Francesca's safety in the balance.

Francesca glared directly at the nearly mad

scientist. "As soon as I get the chance, I'm kicking you right between the eyes."

"Riiiiight," said Dopler.

Zak unfastened the QT wristwatch and handed it over. Dopler instantly brightened.

"Yeah, come to papa, baby. I am *so* out of here . . ."

Dopler removed his "gun," which turned out to be his index finger, and pressed the bezel button on the watch.

Nothing happened.

He took a closer look at the crystal, his expression sinking like a flat tire. "Oh, dude . . . you got it wet."

WHACK!

Francesca delivered an encore performance of her nose-crunching ballet move, as promised.

"Oww," said Dopler as he teetered. "She's limber . . ."

One second later he fell face-first into the garbage, as unconscious as a log.

"Bravo," applauded Zak. Francesca curtsied.

When Dopler came to, he was propped up against a faux-maple headboard in the Sleepy Time Motor Inn, an establishment that boasted free ice with every room. Zak was performing his version of the Spanish Inquisition on him.

"So, if you didn't kidnap my dad, how do you know where he is?"

"Because I saw the dudes from QT snag him, man!"

"Should I kick him again?" queried Francesca as she stepped from the bathroom.

"We'll see," replied Zak, hoping he sounded sufficiently menacing.

Dopler figured that Zak and the ballet-ninja were not a serious threat, at least compared to his former employer. Even so, he decided he had nothing to lose by telling them everything at this point. Dopler owed it to Zak in a way—after all, he got his family into this mess.

"Look, Gates needed to replace me. He has to get this aging problem fixed before the Feds shut him down."

"What aging problem?"

"Look at me, man! I'm not even thirty yet and I'm already full-on grandpa material! Hypertime doesn't just make you *go* faster, it makes you *age* faster, too."

"He's lying," interjected Francesca. "*We* haven't gotten any older."

"You haven't been in long enough," countered the graying scientist. "Anyway, Gates needs your pops to finish this ion stabilizer thingy that counteracts cellular damage, which wouldn't be so bad if they weren't making him work in hypertime."

It took a few seconds for Dopler's last statement to fully register. When it did, Zak went pale.

"You're saying that my dad's locked up in some lab, getting older by the second?"

Dopler slowly nodded back.

Zak sank into a chair, a wave of guilt knocking

him off his feet. Their last night together was spent arguing over a car, something that now seemed utterly selfish and insignificant. Not only that, his dad had tried to patch things up before he left for the convention—and what did Zak tell him? *Have fun with your science friends.*

Zak felt, with a sickening dread, it could end up being the last thing he ever said to him.

They had to save him quick . . . if it wasn't already too late.

FIFTEEN

"I'm sorry, Zakman. It's got me bummin', too," commiserated Dopler. "Your dad was like a father to me."

"Oh yeah, right," Zak said with disgust. "Which is why you're in such a hurry to get to Costa Rica."

"No fair, man! When I sent your dad that watch, I had no idea Gates was gonna bogart everything from the Feds."

To Dopler's credit, this was true. Nevertheless, Zak's father was being held prisoner and was quickly deteriorating thanks to Dopler having involved him.

Zak paced around the cramped motel room. Pointing fingers would accomplish nothing. It was time to get pragmatic.

"Okay . . . there's got to be something we can do to get my dad out of there . . ."

"We?" whined Dopler.

"Yeah, *we*," Zak firmly replied. "I can't go to the police. And since you and my dad were *so close*, I thought maybe you'd like to help."

Dopler looked back sheepishly. "I didn't say we were *that* close."

Zak was fed up and got in Dopler's face.

"Then maybe I'll just drop you off at QT Labs. I'm sure Gates would *love* to have you back."

Dopler knew he was between a headboard and a hard place. Plus, he actually did feel some responsibility. He found himself slowly nodding.

"You win, man."

Zak took off the watch and handed it to him. "Can you fix this?"

Dopler gave it the once-over. Its face was clouded with condensation and there was no numeric display. The scientist sighed.

"Maybe. But we're going to need some stuff you can't get at Radio Shack."

Francesca listened to their bickering for a moment and grabbed her car keys. In her mind, the time for talk was over. "You heard the man—let's get shopping."

A huge banner hung over the entrance to the Kingston Hotel's exposition hall: CONGRESS OF APPLIED SCIENCE—WELCOME!

Close to one hundred booths were geometrically

arranged inside the skylighted courtyard. It was science-geek heaven, with displays covering everything from robotics to genetics to space travel.

Zak, Francesca and Dopler, incognito in sunglasses and hats, strolled up to the ticket booth at the hall entrance.

"Hi!" said the perky convention worker wearing ultra-thick prescription glasses. "Day passes for the expo hall are fourteen dollars, please."

Zak patted his pockets, though he already knew what he'd find—lint. He turned to Dopler.

"Do you have any cash?"

Dopler frowned in a big way.

"You can't ask your hostage for money, man."

Francesca shook her head and pulled out her credit card. The convention worker cheerfully swiped it through the reader.

Now armed with passes, they began to cruise the displays. Dopler had a shopping list that included jeweler's tools, microchips, a magnifying lamp and a mini torch welder. While some of the items were provided in freebie sample bags, most of what he needed had to be "borrowed" from the exhibits. This meant creative distraction, which came easily to Francesca.

"Excuse me, what does this do?" she cooed to a pair of twenty-something nimrods baby-sitting a nebulous Silicon Valley booth. The two young men who shopped for their clothes at "Geeks R Us" gazed at the beauty with their mouths identically agape.

"Uh, it's a transducer with microfilament

circuitry that deciphers digital satellite transmissions for handheld gaming systems," said the tall one.

"With no artifacts," his shorter partner chimed in.

"Wow," she said, thoroughly impressed.

"Would you like to touch it?" said the tall nimrod.

"We don't let just anybody, you know," finished the short one.

"I'd love to."

He placed the generic-looking microchip in her hand and she acted duly blown away.

While Francesca captivated them, Dopler reached into their booth and extracted a mini welding torch off their workbench. Seeing that the mission had been accomplished, Francesca thanked them and made a quick exit.

"Don't get many of those," said the short nimrod as he loosened the top button on his plaid shirt.

A half hour later, they had collected all sorts of electronics. Dopler took a final inventory and nodded.

"All right, man, now I just need someplace quiet to work for a few minutes."

Zak peered around and then smiled. He was looking in the direction of a booth labeled: *PSEUDO SOY! BIOENGINEERED TO FEED THE WORLD!*

What had caught his eye was the small handwritten note taped beneath the sign—GONE TO LUNCH.

The curtains were closed around the exhibit, which provided just the privacy they needed.

They strolled their way over and disappeared inside the booth. Francesca kept an eye out as Zak hovered over Dopler. In less than five minutes, the frazzled inventor had the watch bezel removed and the core of the device clamped in place under a magnifier. Zak watched with fascination as Dopler carefully welded connections on the micro-sized circular motherboard.

"Hey, while you're at it, is there any way to make that watch go faster?" queried Zak.

"What is it with you wacky kids today?" groaned the scientist. "Nothing's ever fast enough." He turned back to the watch just as the welding torch went out.

"Beautiful . . . out of gas," he said as he stood. "I guess I'll have to get another cartridge . . ."

"Sit down, I'll get it."

Zak still wasn't sure if Dopler might try to bolt. "Keep an eye on him," he whispered to Francesca.

Zak slipped from the booth and procured another welding cartridge from the nimrods, who were busy yakking up a potential backer. On the way back, his eyes fell on the logo of the university where his father taught. Zak walked around the corner for a better look and stopped dead in his tracks.

A life-size poster of his dad was hanging over the exhibit, which featured several of his inventions, along with innovations from his top graduate students.

Zak felt a sudden rush of pride for his father.

"He's amazing, isn't he?" said the grad student manning the booth. "Do you know him?"

Zak took in the poster, along with his father's inventions. He suddenly realized how little he knew about his dad's work. Zak felt ashamed for being so self-centered, but he also felt wounded. *Why didn't he involve me more in his projects?*

"I've seen him around," Zak finally said.

As he walked away, it passed through his mind that he and his father could've collaborated on some very cool stuff. Now, more than anything, Zak wanted a second chance with his dad.

While awaiting Zak's return, Dopler had passed the time by drawing an amazingly detailed blueprint of QT Laboratories on a napkin. When Zak arrived with the torch fuel, he and Francesca studied the map while Dopler finished repairing the watch.

"Okay, the side entrance is too obvious, we'll never get through there . . ."

"I still can't believe he drew this," she said.

"Sorry it's so rough," interjected Dopler, not looking up from the magnifier. "I didn't have my protractor."

They gave him a look, then turned back to his incredibly accurate rendering.

"There's gotta be a way in," continued Zak. "Let's just step back, look at the options . . ."

"You're starting to sound like your dad, man—

"Look, man, I need a vacation *real* bad." —Dopler

"Let's just say, *hypothetically*, it was possible to accelerate your molecular structure until the rest of the world seemed as if it were standing still . . ." —Professor Gibbs

"Foreign girl in a foreign land . . . all lonely and vulnerable. I read about this in *Cosmo*." —Zak Gibbs

"That's Francesca, the new girl from *Venezuelaaa*." —Meeker

"Would it be such a stretch for some of your plans to include me?" —Zak

"You know, we could have some serious fun with this thing." —Zak

"Where's that watch? And don't lie, 'cause you're coming with us." —Gates

Zak: "What are we doing?"

Francesca: "A little dance lesson."

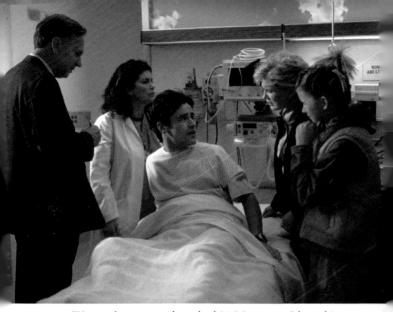

"You stole a van and crashed it! Mom, can I have his room while he's in jail?" —Kelly Gibbs

"We're going to need some stuff you can't get at Radio Shack." —Dopler

"If you went through what I've been through, this place would give you the willies, too." —Dopler

"We're just about to see if your dad's really as brilliant as everyone says he is." —Gates

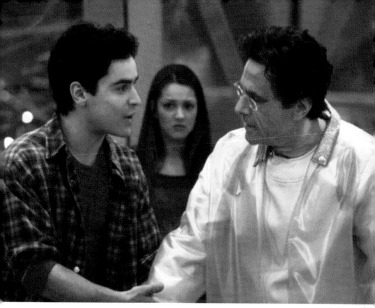

"We've got to put Gates out of business." —Zak

"Hey, Creepy. Nice ride. I hear you're a big hero now."
—Kelly

Jesse Bradford portrays Zak Gibbs.

Jesse performs some high-flying stunts.

Paula Garces (Francesca) and Jesse take a break during filming.

'Let's step back and look at our options . . .'"

"Shut up, I'm nothing like him," Zak blurted.

"It's a compliment, man. Don't blow your RAM."

Not wanting to deal with his emotions, Zak returned to the matter at hand.

"Wait a minute . . . what's under here?" He pointed to the bottom left corner of the napkin-map.

"It's a sewer, right?"

"Ventilation," corrected Dopler.

"Can we get in that way?"

"I guess, if you don't mind being Ginsu-ed by the intake fan."

Zak exhaled and studied the map for the hundredth time. His pupils came back to that ventilation fan.

"Are you positive there's no other way in?"

Dopler nodded soberly. He extinguished the welder and turned off the magnifying light.

"Where's the new watch case?"

Zak pulled out a brand new dive watch he'd bought at a nearby drugstore using Francesca's credit card. By all appearances, it was identical to the hypertime watch.

"Perfecto," smiled Dopler. He popped off the back of the new watch and removed its guts, then carefully lifted the repaired hypertime mechanism and placed it inside the new housing. Dopler pressed a combination of buttons and the luminescent-green display sprang to life, including the QT logo.

"All that technology, incognito," smiled the scientist, verbally patting himself on the back.

Dopler's bloodshot eyes narrowed as he gazed at his invention. The watch was working again . . . and *he* was holding it. His thumb instinctively moved to the button on the left side of the bezel.

Zak snatched the watch away a split second before Dopler pressed the button. "I'll take that, thank you."

"Fine, man," retorted Dopler. "Can't even give a dude time to admire his work."

Dopler tossed the old QT watch housing into a trash can, along with the discarded workings of the new one.

"What are you doing?" chided Zak. "I can sell this stuff on eBay." He dug out the parts and popped the new watch's guts into the old QT housing. "See? Good as new."

Zak pocketed it, then glimpsed through the curtains. All clear.

"Let's get on the road."

Six hours and three hundred miles later, the threesome was sneaking around the back of X-Dream Sports. Being a Sunday night, the store was dark and empty.

Zak moved to the rear door and knocked, Francesca at his side. Dopler lagged behind, struggling with a tank of liquid nitrogen he'd acquired at the convention. Within seconds the heavily bolted door opened, revealing Meeker.

"I got down here as soon as I could after you called," Meeker whispered as he let them in.

Zak moved directly toward the paintball section. "We'll need guns. Lots of guns."

Zak grabbed a pair of paint pistols and stuck them in his waistband. Meeker shook his head with disapproval, then pulled a curtain to reveal a hidden display case. The mother of all paintball guns hung on the wall. He lifted it off its support hooks and handed it to Zak as if it were the Holy Grail.

"You the *man*," praised Zak, slinging it over his shoulder.

At the same time, Francesca was collecting boxes of paint pellets. Their plan was to drain the paint and refill the pellets with liquid nitrogen. The end result would be anti-hypertime weaponry that would hopefully rival their opposition when they broke into QT Labs.

The idea for the guns had come from Zak. Dopler started to say that it was exactly the kind of thing Zak's old man might've cooked up, but decided against it.

Over the next few hours, Francesca and Zak sucked out the paint with syringes and handed the pellets to Dopler as if they were on an assembly line. Wearing protective Teflon gloves, Dopler injected the balls with N_2 from a syringe he had jury-rigged to the nitrogen tank. Dopler quickly placed the finished ammo in the paintball gun magazines, which the trio had modified into mini-refrigerators with foil insulation and coolant packs. The end result looked like a weapon that Will Smith might use on nasty aliens.

"Très cool," nodded Meeker, who had been keeping watch while the others worked.

"This just may work, Zakman," agreed Dopler.

SIXTEEN

Dawn came at QT Laboratories, with a light fog shrouding the low-rise complex. A sole security guard manned the main gate as another walked the perimeter corridor. Otherwise, all was quiet.

"Over here, man," whispered Dopler. He motioned Zak and Francesca behind a grassy knoll just outside the compound. "No security cameras until you get around the corner."

Zak and Francesca followed him stealth-like, both armed with their homemade weaponry and backpacks filled with extra ammo.

Dopler saw something and shoved their heads down. The guard patrolling the perimeter came into view, glanced in their direction, and continued his beat. As soon as he was gone, Dopler jogged over the knoll to a square metal grate. He pulled it up and quickly lowered himself down, Zak and Francesca right behind.

They dropped into a massive concrete chamber, large enough to hold a truck. The sound of a humming motor echoed from somewhere ahead. A trickle of murky fluid flowed beneath their feet.

"Is this stuff toxic?" grimaced Francesca, trying not to step in it.

"Probably," answered Dopler.

He led them in the direction of the hum, the dim light brightening a few lumens. A slight breeze began to move his gray locks.

"We're almost there," Dopler told them, his anxiety growing with every step. They came to a junction and saw what Dopler had drawn on the napkin.

The exhaust fan was much bigger than they had expected, with a diameter of at least six feet. It was also spinning faster than they'd been led to believe.

"This is it," stated Dopler. His voice was unsteady. "Just past here are the ducts into the building."

They stared at the fan soberly, its sharp blades slicing through the damp air in a blur. Just as Zak started to question the plausibility of their plan, Francesca took hold of his wrist, as well as Dopler's.

"Push the button, Zak."

Her positive expression injected him with confidence. He reached down and activated the watch. The rippling flashed through all of them. The liquid beneath their feet was now ice-still. More importantly, the fan had slowed to a crawl.

Zak studied it carefully. While the blades were razor sharp, there appeared to be enough space in their rotations to pass through.

He mustered all the confidence his constricted larynx would allow.

"All right, let's go."

Dopler just stood there.

"C'mon, Earl—you won't fit through the blades with your pack on," said Zak. Somehow "Earl" didn't sound right, but Zak felt they had been through enough together to be on a first-name basis.

Dopler pulled off his backpack and tossed it at Zak's feet. "Here's extra ammo. This is as far as I go."

Zak burned him with a stare. "Hey, we had a deal."

"Look man . . . I'm scared, 'kay? If you went through what I've been through, this place would give you the willies too. I can't go in there, Zakman."

Zak was livid. "He was like a father to you, huh?"

"Hey, that's low, man. If you hadn't taken the watch to begin with, he wouldn't be in here!"

"What are you talking about, you greasy loser? You put my whole family at risk when you sent him that watch!" Zak changed his voice to a Dopleresque whine: "'*I didn't know it was a weapon, I thought it was for science, man.*'"

"That's the truth, man!"

"Yeah? I'll tell you the truth . . ." Zak stepped

closer, his heart in his throat. "That man in there gave his life to students like you! He treated you like a son, you said so yourself! And now that he needs something back, it's too much for you! Well, I *am* his son. And *I'm* going in there."

Although Zak wasn't aware of it, tears were welling in his eyes.

Dopler was moved, no question, but he held his ground. The only way he was going back into Quantum Tech was kicking and screaming.

Francesca glared at Dopler, then tossed their backpacks through the slow-moving blades.

"C'mon, let's go," she quietly said.

Zak took one last look at the scientist, whose eyes were full of fear. He suddenly realized he was just as scared. That he might very well die trying to save his father. That Francesca was facing the same possible fate.

Zak shoved all of these doubts into the background as he jumped between the steel-edged blades.

SEVENTEEN

Zak landed safely on the other side. He then guided Francesca through the sharp blades, being extremely careful not to bump the watch, which would send the massive fan into its deadly spin again if real time resumed. Once she made it past the danger zone, Zak's eyes fell on Dopler, who remained in the outer chamber.

The scientist's look back was conflicted. He didn't feel good about bailing on them . . . but in his mind, he had no choice. Dopler wordlessly retreated, leaving Zak and Francesca on their own.

A maze of concrete corridors funneled into the chamber that Zak and Francesca now occupied. Her eyes darted across all the choices, none of which looked appealing.

"Which one do we take?"

Zak unfolded the napkin map, now frayed at the edges. He studied it carefully for several seconds.

"The tunnel on the left," he finally answered, his voice decisive. In truth, he wasn't 100 percent positive this was right, but he remembered a saying his father had told him when he'd been waffling about which paint color to use on his Mustang model: *He who hesitates is lost.* Zak had followed his gut and chosen hi-gloss red, never regretting it.

This time he chose the left tunnel. And prayed for the same result.

Somewhere above Zak and Francesca sat the Quantum Tech lobby, a vast, sterile interior with mirror-like walls of black granite and brushed aluminum elevators. A pair of security guards sat behind an imposing reception desk filled with surveillance monitors. On one screen, a suited executive was marching from an elevator with his harried assistants in tow. Another showed an express courier rushing down a corridor to make her deadline.

All of them, including the guards, were frozen in place.

A metal floor vent began to jiggle. The vent cracked open a few inches and two pairs of eyes came into view—Zak's and Francesca's. They took in the lobby from floor level. Although it was a bit premature for self-congratulations, Zak's choice of routes was a good one. Better still, they appeared to be the only ones in hypertime.

"Let's go," he said assuredly, pushing the vent all the way open.

An alarm immediately sounded—in hypertime *and* real time.

Zak and Francesca froze. Gates's security system was more advanced than they had assumed. But there was no turning back now.

Dopler was climbing from the grate outside QT Labs when he heard the distant echo of the alarm. He knew what this meant: Zak and Francesca had been caught, or would be soon. He'd figured this would be the likely scenario, which is why he didn't join them. Dopler had no intention of being held prisoner again and aging to death inside of Henry Gates's cold metallic laboratory.

So why was he standing there and not running off?

Dopler knew the answer, of course. It was because he actually cared about them. But he also knew there wasn't the slightest chance that he could help them at this point.

Dopler closed his eyes, forced his conscience aside, and continued his retreat.

Henry Gates was hovering over the still-uncompleted ion stabilizer when he heard the alarm, which had a distinct staccato tone. Gates knew exactly what this particular tone meant, as did Richard and Jay. The two agents immediately activated their own watches, rippled, and disappeared into hypertime.

Dopler's map had been detailed enough to get Zak and Francesca inside, but the interior floor plan left much to interpretation. Paintball guns leveled, they moved down the nearly identical hallways like members of a SWAT team. Eventually one of the passages led them to a large central atrium. Natural light filtered down from above, spilling over the steel banister of a spiral staircase that led down to a labyrinth of research rooms.

The two were about to descend the staircase when Zak noticed a reflection in the smooth granite walls. Something was moving, which could only mean one thing—they were not alone in hypertime.

Zak instantly spun around.

POP—POP!

He fired two N_2 pellets at a pair of QT security guards, who quickly dove behind a reception desk. Zak's shots vaporized against the wall, missing them.

Francesca instantly dropped and fired under the desk. One of the guards howled as the liquid nitrogen hit his legs, freezing him from the knees down and holding him in place.

"I'll hold these guys off," she told him, firing off another shot. "You go find your dad!"

Zak wasn't sure if this was a good idea—if these guards were in hypertime, more were sure to follow. Then again, time was of the essence, and he wasn't going anywhere unless Francesca kept these guys pinned down. He made an instinctive decision—

"I'll meet you back at the fan in five minutes!"

Zak rushed to a frozen QT mail boy climbing off his bike just outside the atrium and yanked his transportation away. The bike was no BMX, but Zak Gibbs was no ordinary bicyclist. As Francesca provided cover, he flew down the spiral staircase, letters and packages bouncing out of the bike's saddlebags with every bump.

He was greeted by two more hypertime guards on the lower level, who immediately fired their own, more sophisticated N_2 weapons. Zak recklessly skidded into a research room, barely avoiding their blasts. As the guards sprinted in pursuit, he slalomed around a dozen frozen human obstacles before hopping onto their lab tables. Microscopes and test tubes went crashing as Zak cranked through the room, jumping from one table to the next. He made a final leap from the last table and careened back into the main corridor.

Just ahead was an isolated elevator. He considered blowing past it since he wasn't even sure the elevator would work in hypertime, but a *whooshing* sound drew his glance.

The elevator door slid open vertically.

Zak instinctively locked up the bike, slid across the floor toward the elevator, and pulled up his paintball gun.

POP—POP!

A short, dark-suited QT agent was hit in two places before he stepped out the door. As the man became a statue, Zak slid into the elevator cabin and tossed the borrowed bike into the hall. His vision darted to the access panel. Choosing LEVEL THREE was an easy process of elimination—he'd been on every other level. He quickly punched the button.

"*Restricted access requested. Please step forward for retinal scan.*"

Although the voice was pleasant enough, Zak knew the computerized female would not negotiate. Worse, the guards had just emerged from the research room and were rushing in his direction.

Zak glanced at the frozen agent and came up with a desperate but brilliant solution. He jockeyed the stocky man over to the access panel and pressed his face against the retinal scanner. The cone-shaped laser splashed across the agent's pupils, then disappeared.

"*Have a nice day . . . Frank Yamada.*"

WHOOSH.

The elevator door slid down and Zak began to descend.

"Thanks, Frank," he told the inanimate man as he eased him onto the elevator floor.

As Zak glided to a stop at LEVEL THREE, he knew something was wrong before the door had even opened. There was a scuffling sound just beyond it.

Zak readied his gun.

WHOOSH.

The door rose, revealing Francesca. Zak lowered his weapon and started to smile . . . until he realized she was rock-still.

"Hello, Zachary."

Gates stepped into view, flanked by Richard and Jay.

White icy pain engulfed Zak as they fired their N_2 weapons point-blank.

When the fog cleared, Zak was standing as still as Francesca. Gates unstrapped Zak's watch and slipped it into his coat pocket. He stared into the teenager's blank eyes.

"Can't thank you enough for bringing this back," he grinned.

EIGHTEEN

As Zak plunged back into real time, he glanced down and saw the watch magically vanish from his wrist. The next thing he felt was teeth-jarring speed as invisible forces whisked him into the heart of QT Laboratories. Francesca got the same treatment.

When their shivering bodies came to a stop, they were standing opposite the ion stabilizer. The futuristic-looking chair was nearly complete, with a trio of technicians busily programming it. A split second later, Gates and his cohorts disengaged from hypertime and materialized beside the chair.

"Where's my dad?" Zak instantly demanded. When Gates didn't answer, Zak began to call out, his voice reverberating throughout the immense lab—

"DAD! DAD!"

Gates smiled. The kid had some guts, no question.

"In there," he finally replied. Gates nodded at the Clean Room, which stood thirty feet away on its metal stage. "We're just about to see if he's really as brilliant as everyone says he is."

Zak broke free and ran to the Clean Room. Gates made no gesture to have him stopped. Instead, he strolled in the same direction, with Richard and Jay roughly escorting Francesca.

Zak arrived outside the Clean Room and gazed inside, but it was empty. Suddenly the room was filled with a burst of N_2. As the cryogenic fog cleared, Zak felt an excruciating vacuum suck out his insides.

"No . . ."

His dad became visible in the center of the room. The circular platform was in its raised position, with Professor Gibbs slumped opposite the huge monitor that occupied it. The 3-D rendition of the ion stabilizer stared back at him. Pages and pages of handwritten equations were spread everywhere. The professor's head was buried in his hands as he struggled to solve an impossible equation—a problem that was slowly claiming his own life. Even facing away, his body posture told the story: He was *older*.

Gates stepped beside the stunned seventeen-year-old.

"You know, he must be very fond of you," he taunted. "I couldn't get him to do a damn thing until I threatened to kill you."

Gates nodded to a technician, who released the

hatch into the Clean Room. Zak dashed inside. Richard and Jay released Francesca, who immediately followed.

"Dad . . . ?"

Professor Gibbs heard his son's voice like it had been conjured from a dream. He slowly swiveled to face him, thinking he had imagined it.

Again, Zak felt his stomach being twisted, this time tenfold. His father's sideburns had turned gray, the corners of his eyes riddled with crow's feet. Due to the intense concentration and lack of sleep, he was barely coherent.

"Zak . . . ?"

He rose from the chair and hugged his son, regaining much of the energy Gates had drained from him.

Gates stood in the doorway and watched with bemusement at the touching father-son reunion. Dr. Gibbs met his stare.

"You swore you'd leave him out of this!" he shouted at the megalomaniac.

"Don't blame me," shrugged Gates. "He showed up all on his own. Maybe he needs his allowance or something."

Gates took a step backwards and the Clean Room door slammed down, imprisoning Zak and Francesca with Professor Gibbs.

The professor held his son at arm's length. He was thrilled to see him, true enough, but he was equally upset.

"You *came* here?"

"Yeah, well, what was I supposed to do?" Zak answered defensively.

Dr. Gibbs sank back into his chair. "Zak, no, no . . . I was only cooperating with them so they would leave you alone."

"Well, I couldn't just leave you here to die."

"No, you had to come *join* me."

"I don't believe this!" erupted Zak. "You're always saying I only show up when I need something—so now I come here to help, and you don't appreciate that either!"

"I'm sorry, but putting your life in the hands of terrorists is not exactly what I had in mind!"

"I can't do anything right for you! Lucky I'm just your son, and not one of your precious students. Then you'd *really* be disappointed!"

"Would you two stop it?" Francesca broke in. "Geez, you really *are* alike."

The two men, one young, the other aging quickly, abruptly shut up. Professor Gibbs glanced at his son.

"Who's your friend?"

"Francesca. From school," Zak said curtly.

Dad took another look at his son's crush. "No wonder you wanted a car."

Before the argument could resume, a warning alarm sounded. It had a distinctly different tone from the one Zak had triggered earlier.

Gates moved to a security console outside the Clean Room. Zak, Francesca, and Professor Gibbs carefully watched him.

"Who is it?" Gates said tersely into the video intercom.

The security guard at the main gate blinked onto Gates's monitor.

"Agent Moore is here, sir."

Indeed, Agent James Moore from the NSA was waiting at the entrance with a long parade of sleek black SUVs. Moore offered no smile as he faced the security camera outside the guard booth.

"Happy Monday, Mr. Gates. You have some things for me?"

"Oh, right," replied Gates, never breaking his cool. "Listen, sorry for the inconvenience, but I'm going to have to ask you to come back in another hour or so."

"This isn't the prom, Gates," barked Moore, losing his patience straight away. "The agency is serious about this. Now do us both a favor and—"

"You can't come in," interrupted Gates. He switched off the monitor and banished the NSA official from his view.

"Well imagine that," Moore mumbled. Astounded by the man's arrogance, he almost smiled as he lifted his walkie-talkie and sent a message to the long line of vehicles behind him.

"Gentlemen, start your engines."

Over two dozen V-8s revved loudly as they prepared to ram the main gate and take Gates's facility by force.

NINETEEN

From inside the Clean Room, Zak could see a large security monitor displaying a view of the main entrance. The convoy under Agent Moore's command was speeding toward the gate.

"Yes! We're going to get out of here!"

"I wouldn't be so sure," said his father somberly. Professor Gibbs was standing on the other side of the Clean Room, watching as Gates hovered over a group of technicians manning a sinister-looking console crammed with switches, gauges and monitors. Zak and Francesca followed his stare.

"What's that?" asked Zak, though he wasn't sure he wanted to know. Before his father could answer, Gates addressed the entire lab.

"Change of plans, people—we'll be testing the ion stabilizer a little earlier than expected!"

Gates tapped the console's central screen and brought up a complex menu. His finger moved to a touch-sensitive icon that said: HYPERTIME: ENGAGE.

He jabbed it decisively.

A bolt of energy surged from the console like an electrical tidal wave, rippling up the skeletal steel framework that encompassed the secret lab.

"What's he doing?" queried Francesca, her voice shaky. Understandably, she was starting to freak.

"He's taking us *all* into hypertime," answered the professor.

A moment after he said it, the rippling wave engulfed the Clean Room and passed through their bodies.

At this very same nanosecond—

CRASH!

The convoy of SUVs smashed into the guard booth and perimeter fence, and froze halfway through. Shattered pieces of wood, glass and metal hung in midair. Agent Moore glared out from the windshield of the lead SUV, his unflinching expression captured in time.

"No . . ." Zak's eyes were transfixed on the security monitor, which showed the NSA convoy freeze-framed. At the rate they were moving, it would be a long, long time before Moore and his troops came to the rescue.

Simultaneously, Gates was powering up the ion stabilizer. Thanks to Professor Gibbs's number-crunching over the last twenty-four hours, Gates knew the lab's occupants couldn't remain in "global hypertime" for more than a few minutes unless the ion stabilizer was functioning properly.

"Three minutes and counting!" Gates shouted at the technicians who surrounded the stabilizer. As the lab-coats instantly scrambled to finish the programming, Gates rapidly entered keystrokes on his console. The second he finished typing, an ominous digital countdown began flashing across every monitor in the room.

Zak, Francesca, and Dr. Gibbs watched it all from their sterile prison. "You know, once he gets that thing working, he won't need us anymore," uttered Zak.

"They're going to kill us, aren't they?" Francesca said this to no one in particular, and neither Zak nor his father offered an answer. Professor Gibbs, thoroughly drained at this point, had already given up. Zak, however, refused to do so. He began stalking the Clean Room like a caged lion.

"There's got to be another way out of here . . ."

"Zak, I'm telling you, there's no way out," said Professor Gibbs with resignation. "It's sealed tight as a—"

"What's this?" interrupted Zak.

His keen eyes had spotted a small gas valve in the corner, the kind used with Bunsen burners in a high school science lab.

"They've been having me run some experiments with hydrogen," answered the professor.

"Hydrogen . . . ?"

A glimmer of hope brightened Zak's eyes. He'd

learned in fourth-period chemistry that hydrogen gas was highly flammable, very dangerous, and not to be messed with . . . except, of course, when you're planning an elaborate escape.

"You can't use it," said his dad, as if he'd read his mind. "They turn it on from the tanks, out there." He pointed to a cluster of hydrogen tanks outside the Clean Room, cropped against the wall. A sign above them confirmed what Zak had learned in school: EXTREMELY FLAMMABLE—NO SMOKING.

Refusing to let the notion go, Zak continued to gaze at the tanks.

"What are you going to do, blow us up?" asked his dad facetiously.

"Not us . . . *them*," Zak answered, dead serious. He gazed at Gates and his frantic technicians. In a rage of frustration, he lifted the heavy desk chair his father had been occupying and slammed it into the Clean Room windows. The windows flexed but didn't break. Undaunted, Zak kept hammering.

Gates glanced up at the Clean Room, more annoyed than angry. He moved to a security console and punched some keys.

As Zak raised the chair for another blow, thick metal shutters rotated on their servos and completely shielded the Clean Room windows.

"Well, that was effective," sighed Zak, his voice unable to belie their grave situation. He lowered the chair and sat down in it, trying to regroup.

Sensing their time was about to end, Professor Gibbs moved closer to his son.

"Zak . . . I'm sorry I got so caught up in my work."

"Dad, don't." Zak knew this kind of conversation was what people did when they were about to die, and that was *not* going to happen.

"It was never because I care more about my students," continued his father, desperately wanting to make amends. He started to say more, but his eyes told Zak everything the teenager needed to hear. He loved him more than anything in this world.

Zak slowly stood and they hugged for a long time, wordlessly forgiving each other.

Just outside the Clean Room, progress was coming slow for Gates as the seconds ticked down.

"Sir, we've got a problem," said one of the techies in charge of data uploading. "We can't get in—the security codes have been changed."

Gates hurried to the stabilizer display panel. ACCESS DENIED flashed back in his face, as if to mock him. The control-freak head of QT Labs was feeling the onset of a new migraine as he gazed in the direction of the Clean Room.

"Dr. Gibbs!"

Behind the metal shutters, Zak, Francesca and Professor Gibbs were greeted by Gates's beet-red face on a monitor, along with his irate voice.

"We had an agreement," he bellowed. "I let your son live, *if* you cooperate."

"Yeah, well . . . it's time to renegotiate," replied Dr. Gibbs after a thoughtful pause. Some of his son's spunk had rubbed off on him; he now decided he would not go down without a fight.

"My son and the girl go free. *Then* you get the code."

Gates glanced at the countdown. He had less than two minutes to get the ion stabilizer working. There was no time to argue.

"Fine!"

He quickly turned to Richard and Jay. "Get the kids out of here and bring me Dr. Gibbs—now!"

Zak frantically looked around as Richard and Jay made their way toward the Clean Room. He was not about to leave his father behind.

He spotted a flat-head screwdriver near one of the desktop computers. Zak grabbed the tool, hurried to the entrance hatch, and jammed it into the door's track.

"Zak, what are you doing?" whispered his dad in a rush. Only one thing was on his mind—saving his son and Francesca.

"Finishing what I came here to do," Zak stubbornly answered. He reached into his pocket and extracted a wristwatch, strapping it on.

Francesca gazed at the dive watch with the bright yellow bezel.

"But Gates took your watch—I saw him . . ."

"He took *a* watch," clarified Zak, "which he can probably get about ten dollars for on eBay."

Francesca continued to stare with puzzlement.

"I switched them in the elevator," Zak concluded with a grin. Francesca immediately understood and beamed back. Always thinking ahead, Zak had switched the watch case he'd salvaged from the trash with the *real*, repaired QT watch. The clever switch was meant to be insurance, and the time to cash in his policy was now.

He reached for the bezel button.

"Zak, no!"

Professor Gibbs looked positively frantic. "You can't accelerate while you're already *in* hypertime! You'd be going too fast—it could kill you!"

"We've got no choice, Dad. Besides, sometimes you have to close your eyes, grit your teeth and go on faith."

It was the same saying Zak had told his father when he had wanted to buy the Mustang. Zak couldn't remember where he'd heard it—he may have even made it up—but it was a credo he now lived by.

Before his dad could stop him, Zak pressed the watch's button.

TWENTY

A bright white spiderweb of electrical energy crackled over Zak's body. Within seconds, he began to glow. He staggered slightly, overwhelmed by the force pulsating through his flesh. Zak placed his hand on a lab table to steady himself.

His hand passed *through* the table, as if he were a ghost.

Francesca just gazed in disbelief. So did Professor Gibbs—half out of concern, half out of scientific awe.

"Unbelievable . . . your molecules are going so fast, you went right through the table."

To Zak's ears, his father was talking in slow motion. It was like he was in a dream state.

"Aaaaaarrrrrrrre yyyyooouuu ohhhhkaaaayyy?" asked Francesca, her voice also running at half-speed.

"I have no idea," he uttered.

From their perspective, Zak sounded like Alvin and the Chipmunks with a lot of echo.

Francesca reached out to touch his half-transparent face. She pulled back with a start as her fingers sunk beneath his flesh. Still, she *could* feel him, and Zak could feel her as well. Concentrating hard, Zak reached for her hand. At first he couldn't grasp it—his fingers went right through hers—but he closed his eyes and forced himself into slow, steady breathing. He'd watched a special on transcendental meditation once and remembered something about mind over matter, about slowing down your metabolism by eliminating extraneous thoughts.

After ten seconds of methodical breathing and intense concentration, Zak was able to hold Francesca's hand firmly.

One second later, the Clean Room door was grinding against the screwdriver Zak had jammed in the track. Richard and Jay had arrived. Zak's ploy bought them five seconds before the screwdriver snapped and the door scraped open.

Richard stepped in first. He took one look at Zak and knew something was definitely not right. Richard quickly raised his N_2 weapon and blasted him—but Zak avoided it in a blurry flash of speed. As the muscular henchman continued to fire, Zak easily dodged the liquid nitrogen. Richard soon realized he was out-matched and dived out the door, triggering the hatch release before Zak could escape. He jogged back to Gates, who was pacing circles around the ion stabilizer crew. They had just over one minute left on the countdown.

"Sir, we've got a problem in there."

"What kind of problem?" retorted Gates with zero patience.

"I . . . I don't know," stammered Richard. "But that kid is doing something freaky."

Gates stared at the Clean Room. Enough was enough.

"Bring 'em down," he ordered, indicating that they flood the Clean Room with N_2 and send its occupants back into real time.

Meanwhile, Zak had come up with a plan.

"All right . . . everybody knows what to do?"

Francesca nodded, moving to the center of the room.

Professor Gibbs looked at his son with dread, but he found himself nodding as well. Although Zak's plan was far from foolproof, he decided to follow his son's advice and close his eyes, grit his teeth, and act on pure faith. Gibbs picked up a small welding torch from the lab table and ignited it.

Zak stepped forward, stuck his hand against the shutters, and felt his flesh pass through the metal.

Just outside the Clean Room, Richard was about to release the liquid nitrogen and freeze all of them into real time. He didn't see Zak's hand as it magically moved through the shutters, followed by his face. Half of Zak's body was in the Clean Room, half was out. It was as if he were breaking the surface of water, only vertical.

"Hi," he said to Richard.

The brawny man turned around, thoroughly stunned by the eerie apparition. This bought Zak the precious moments he needed to slow down his metabolism and solidify. Before Richard could raise his weapon, Zak grabbed the muscleman and whacked his head against the shutters, knocking him out cold.

Another guard came around the corner just as Zak took out Richard.

"What in the . . . ?"

The teenager was still half in, half out of the Clean Room.

Gates immediately stopped work on the stabilizer and glanced up as well.

"Stop him!"

A half-dozen armed QT guards converged on Zak as he pushed himself all the way through the metal shutters. Concentrating hard, he made a wild leap onto the outside wall of the Clean Room and scaled it like Spiderman. The guards opened fire, but from their perspective he was moving in a blur.

Zak scampered down the other side and spotted the hydrogen tanks. Just as his dad had said, a conduit led directly to the Clean Room. Zak zeroed-in on the control valve just as a group of guards encircled him.

It was now or never.

Zak lunged off the Clean Room catwalk. Before he hit the ground, an icy cloud of liquid nitrogen hit him hard . . . fired by Henry Gates.

Zak was abruptly shocked out of "hyper-hypertime" into regular hypertime as he landed. He was now moving at the same speed as his nemesis. Zak rolled over to the hydrogen tanks, threw the control valve open, and clawed his way beneath a metal walkway.

A high-pressure hissing sound came as the gas rushed through the conduit toward the Clean Room.

Gates didn't know exactly what Zak was up to, but the hiss told him it wasn't good. His beady eyes rolled to the Clean Room, where its occupants could not be seen due to the closed shutters. Gates immediately disengaged the shields.

The room appeared to be empty. Worse, there was a small flame—the welding torch—propped up in the center of the room.

A sickening dread swallowed Gates as he comprehended what was about to happen. His mouth slowly fell open.

"This is why I never had kids . . ."

KABOOM!!!

The Clean Room exploded in a fanfare of smoke, shrapnel and glass, knocking Gates and his underlings flat on their backs.

TWENTY-ONE

Zak crawled from beneath the walkway as a dusty haze settled over the lab. He took a quick look around. No one was moving.

He trampled through the rubble to the sparse remains of the Clean Room. Its walls were gone, along with the furniture and expensive equipment. Essentially all that remained was the floor. His father and Francesca were nowhere to be seen.

Zak's heart skipped a beat. They'd been allowed all of sixty seconds to plan this, so there was plenty of room for error.

The hum of a hydraulic lift ushered in a sigh of relief. The circular platform at the room's center began to rise, bringing with it his father and Francesca, who were safely tucked beneath it. All three embraced as they took in the disaster, thankful to have survived.

"Let's get out of here," said Zak, not wanting to push their luck. They climbed over the debris and made their way toward the elevator, passing what was left of the main security console.

Ten steps later, Gates rose from behind it.

"Freeze," he said in a casual tone.

Francesca was the first to turn.

WHOOSH!

Gates fired a powerful blast of N_2, hitting her squarely. Francesca stopped dead in her tracks, shocked back into real time. Gates smiled at Zak next, who had no retreat.

"Say good night, little man."

POP—POP—POP!

Gates looked down to see several splotches of liquid nitrogen spreading across his suit.

"Good night, little man," a familiar voice sarcastically replied.

POP—POP—POP—POP!

Earl Dopler stepped from the shadows and pummeled Gates with another flurry of N_2 pellets. Gates screamed with each direct hit, his body painfully being frozen in sections.

"Hurts, doesn't it?" Dopler jeered.

Gates didn't answer. He was stiff as a board, a look of agony captured on his face.

Zak looked at Dopler long and hard. Whatever he might've previously thought about the wacko scientist, he now viewed him with plenty of respect.

"Glad you could make it," Zak smiled.

Agent Moore and his convoy finally arrived after Professor Gibbs had disengaged the "global hypertime" that Gates had used on the lab's occupants, returning everyone to a normal unaccelerated state. Zak, Francesca, Gibbs and Dopler watched with satisfaction as the government agents took everyone into custody, Agent Moore personally arresting Henry Gates. By the time they finished, a half-dozen hypertime watches had been confiscated, along with all of Gates's research.

Francesca slipped her arm through Zak's as they emerged from the mess. "Remember that day you asked if I wanted to get a cup of coffee sometime?"

"Yeah," he nodded with a weary smile.

"Now would be good."

His grin widened as they stepped into the elevator.

Professor Gibbs and Dopler were right on their heels, also thrilled to have survived the amazing ordeal. Dr. Gibbs brushed splinters and dust off his jacket as he joined Zak and Francesca in the elevator.

"Dopler, do me a favor—next time you need help on your math homework . . . don't call me."

Dopler's wrinkled face formed a sly grin. He was about to join them when something coaxed a glance back into the lab.

The ion stabilizer was still sitting intact, all its monitors aglow.

"Hey, Dr. G.—did you ever get this anti-aging gizmo working? I don't want to stay like this forever."

"Forget it, Dopler—I never had a chance to test it."

It went in one ear and out the other as the elevator doors closed, leaving Dopler behind.

Now alone, Dopler moved toward the stabilizer like a moth drawn to flame. He slipped into its big comfortable chair and gazed up at the complicated control panel.

It beckoned him to give it a try.

TWENTY-TWO

If Jenny Gibbs had panicked when her son disappeared, she'd nearly lost her mind when her husband went missing as well. More than a day had passed, with no word on his or Zak's whereabouts. Adding to her anguish was Detective Freemont, who had offered interrogation instead of help and comfort. The situation was serious enough that even Kelly was worried.

So, when the melodic chime of their doorbell finally came, it brought massive relief. Her husband had called with the good news that he and Zak were on their way home, but Mrs. Gibbs wouldn't rest until she saw them in the flesh.

She could see her husband's outline silhouetted in the door's stained glass as she rushed to open it.

She barely gave him a glance as she fell into his arms, her whole body draining with relief.

"Thank God you're okay . . ."

She hugged him another few seconds, then held him at arm's length and took in his face. Professor Gibbs had shaved and cleaned himself up, but he still had flecks of gray in his temples and a few new wrinkles. Mrs. Gibbs ran her fingers across the crow's feet near his eyes.

"What's this?"

"It's okay," he said calmly. "I'm just . . . a little more distinguished, that's all." In truth, he felt fine, and in some ways, better than he had in years. He knew he was extremely fortunate to be alive, and had a new lease on life.

"Where's Zak?" asked Mrs. Gibbs, looking around with some concern.

"Oh, uh . . . we had to make a little stop, but he should be here any minute. Don't worry, he's fine."

Just then, Kelly came flying in from the backyard.

"Daddy!"

She threw her arms around her father, which quickly turned into a group hug.

The throaty rumble of a 289-cubic-inch V8-engine turned their heads. Zak's dream car cruised into view, the afternoon sunlight splashing across the Mustang's cherry-red hood. Zak was behind the wheel, smiling as wide as his cheeks would allow. Francesca was riding shotgun. Somebody was stretched out in the backseat, though it was hard to tell who.

Zak pulled up, hopped out, and injected himself in the family embrace as they hurried to meet him.

"Hey, creepy—nice ride," said Kelly as she self-consciously hugged her brother. "I hear you're a big hero now."

"Well . . . I don't know about hero," he answered modestly.

"Hey, I'm not going to be nice all day, so enjoy it."

Zak grinned as his mother pulled him into another hug.

"Oh, Zak, honey . . ."

He glanced at Francesca and rolled his eyes. Mrs. Gibbs sensed her son's embarrassment and released him.

"You must be Francesca," she offered with a sweet smile.

"Nice to meet you," replied the teenager, offering her hand from the passenger seat. Zak's mother spontaneously leaned over the door and gave her a hug instead.

Mom then noticed the boy in the backseat. He looked to be about thirteen, with sandy blond hair and blue eyes.

"Who's this?"

Zak and his dad traded a look. Dr. Gibbs stepped forward and cleared his throat.

"Oh, um, actually, there's something I forgot to

tell you on the phone. We had a little problem down at the lab."

"Yeah, we may have some company for awhile," interjected Zak.

The kid in the backseat smiled at Mrs. Gibbs. "Hey, Mrs. G.—how's it hanging?"

The voice was unmistakable.

"Dopler . . . ?" said Mrs. Gibbs, more than a little bewildered.

Kelly stepped forward and got a good look at him, her eyes mooning.

"Hel-lo gorgeous."

She immediately jumped into the backseat beside him.

"Oh, no—whoa!" yelled Zak.

"I don't think so," chimed in Professor Gibbs.

"Hit it!" squealed Kelly. "Let's see what this thing can do!"

She threw an arm around thirteen-year-old Dopler with a big grin. Zak and Francesca couldn't help laughing.

Zak took one last look at his parents, his eyes lingering on his father. They shared a moment that spoke of where they had started, what they had lost, and where they had finally arrived. They exchanged a poignant nod, then Zak's foot found the throttle.

Just as they zoomed off, a shiny reflection winked back from his left wrist.

Detective Freemont was pulling up with a fresh arsenal of questions as Zak roared down the residential street. He immediately flipped on his siren and gave pursuit.

He could only rub his eyes when the Mustang seemed to ripple, and then vanish in an inexplicable blur.

ABOUT THE AUTHORS

Rob Hedden has written, produced, and directed movies, long-form television, TV series, and documentaries since 1984. In addition to the *Clockstoppers* screenplay, he wrote and directed *Friday the 13th Part VIII: Jason Takes Manhattan*; *The Colony*, starring John Ritter and Hal Linden; *Dying To Live*, starring Jonathan Frakes; and *Alien Fury* starring WWF star Chyna. Additionally, he wrote and produced the network movies *When the Cradle Falls*; *Simon & Simon: Together Again*; and *The Return of Ironside*; directed the films *Any Place but Home* and *Kidnapped in Paradise* for the USA network; directed the ABC series *The Commish* and the syndicated *Friday the 13th: The Series*. He has also written for *MacGyver*, *SeaQuest DSV*, and the revival of *Alfred Hitchcock Presents*. He is currently directing *Enterprise*, the new Star Trek series.

Rob lives in Laguna Beach, California with his wife and three sons, and surfs when the waves are good.

Andy Hedden began his writing career at age seven. It was the first day of second grade and the teacher asked the class to write a theme entitled: "What I Did On My Summer Vacation." Try as he might, Andy couldn't find anything about that summer worth writing about, so he made up a story about going deep-sea diving for giant pearls. Accompanying the text was a crayon illustration of the author prying open a clam the size of a washing machine while being menaced by a monstrous squid.

Andy has loved telling tall tales ever since. He has collaborated on several film and TV projects with his brother, Rob, including the original screen story for *Clockstoppers*, *Simon & Simon: Together Again*, and *Strange Luck*. He has also acted in over twenty stage and television productions and performed as a drummer.

Andy lives in Laguna Beach, California, with his dog, Ginger. When not writing, acting, and playing music, he indulges in hard labor at the beach.